headwork class

GW01072029

Oliver Twist

CHARLES DICKENS
adapted by Chris Culshaw

OXFORD
UNIVERSITY PRESS

1 ∾ OLIVER'S BIRTH

Oliver Twist began life in the town workhouse*. There were no loving grandparents or anxious aunts present at the birth. There was no proud father at the bedside. There was no one, except the parish* doctor and the old woman from the workhouse who helped him.

Oliver had trouble breathing. The doctor thought he might die at first.

When Oliver started to cry his mother said, 'Let me see the child once before I die.'

'You must not talk of dying,' said the doctor.

'Lord bless her heart, no!' said the old woman. 'When you've had thirteen children and you're as old as me, then you can talk about dying.'

Oliver's mother shook her head. She stretched out her hand towards the child. The doctor put the baby in her arms. She kissed Oliver once with her cold white lips. Then she fell back and died.

'It's all over,' said the doctor.

'Oh, poor girl, so it is,' said the old woman.

'She was a good-looking girl too. Where did she come from?'

'She was found lying in the street, last night. She must have walked a long way. Her shoes were worn to pieces.'

The doctor leaned over the girl's body. He looked at the left hand. 'The old story,' he said, shaking his head sadly, 'no wedding ring.'

When the doctor left, the old woman took the baby over to the fire and dressed him. He cried very loudly. If he had known that he was a parish child*, and a workhouse orphan*, he would have cried even louder.

Oliver spent the first nine years of his life in the smaller, children's workhouse, three miles from the adult workhouse where he had been born. An elderly woman, called Mrs Mann, was in charge of him and the other orphan boys. The parish gave Mrs Mann sevenpence-halfpenny* a week for each boy. Mrs Mann starved the boys and kept most of the money for herself. She beat and bullied them. The boys were often ill from the hunger and the cold. Oliver was pale and thin, like the others.

One day Mr Bumble, the beadle*, came to see Mrs Mann.

'Why, Mr Bumble,' she said, showing him into the parlour*, 'how glad I am to see you.'

'I am here on business, Mrs Mann – parish business,' he said. He put his cocked hat* and cane* on the table and sat down.

'Now, will you take a little drop of something, Mr Bumble?' asked Mrs Mann.

'No, not a drop.'

'Just a little drop?'

'What is it?'

'Gin. I always keep a little in the house, in case one of the dear children is poorly. I don't like to see them suffer, Mr Bumble.'

Mrs Mann gave the beadle a glass of gin and water.

'You are a very kind woman. You are like a mother to those boys. I drink to your health.'

Mr Bumble took out a pocket-book*. 'And now to business. The child Oliver Twist is nine years old today.'

'Bless him,' said Mrs Mann.

'The parish offered a reward of twenty pounds for information about the boy, but we have never been able to find out anything about his mother or father.'

'What about his name?' said Mrs Mann. 'Who gave him that?'

'I did. I name all the foundlings* in alphabetical order. The last was an S. I named him Swubble. So this one was a T. Twist. Now that he's nine, he's too old to stay here. He's to be moved back into the adult house. The board* has sent me to fetch him.'

When they got to the adult workhouse the beadle took Oliver into a large whitewashed room. Eight or ten fat gentlemen were sitting around a large table.

'Bow to the board, Oliver!' said Mr Bumble.

Mr Limbkins, the chairman* of the board, spoke to Oliver. 'What's your name, boy?'

Oliver had tears in his eyes. He was too frightened to speak.

A gentleman in a white waistcoat* said, 'He's a fool.'

'Boy,' said Mr Limbkins, 'listen to me. You do know that you are an orphan, I suppose?'

'What's that, sir?' said Oliver.

'What did I tell you?' said the gentleman in the white waistcoat. 'The boy is a fool.'

'Hush!' said Mr Limbkins. 'Oliver, you know you've got no mother or father? You know that you were brought up by the parish, don't you?'

'Yes, sir,' replied Oliver, weeping bitterly.

'You have come here to be educated and taught a useful trade*,' said Mr Limbkins. He turned to the beadle. 'That will be all, Mr Bumble. Take the boy away.'

Oliver was led away to a large dim ward*. There, on a rough hard bed, he sobbed himself to sleep.

The boys were fed in a long stone hall. At one end of the hall the master stood next to a large copper* full of gruel*. Each boy was given one small bowl of gruel. The bowls never needed washing. The boys polished them with their spoons till they shone. Then they sucked their fingers.

Oliver and the other boys suffered the pains of slow starvation for three months. Then one day they decided that somebody should ask for more gruel. They drew lots*, and Oliver drew the short straw.

That evening the boys took their places in the dining hall. The gruel was served and eaten. Oliver was terrified, but reckless* with hunger. He rose from the table, bowl in hand, and walked up to the master.

'Please, sir, I want some more.'

The master, a fat, red-faced man, turned very pale. He gazed in astonishment at the boy.

'What!' he said, in a faint voice.

'Please, sir, I want some more.'

The master hit Oliver with the ladle*, grabbed him by the arm, and called for the beadle.

The next day Mr Bumble told the board what had happened. 'Mr Limbkins, sir, Oliver Twist has asked for more!'

'That boy will be hung,' said the gentleman in the white waistcoat.

The next morning a notice was pasted on the outside of the workhouse gate. It offered a reward of five pounds to anyone who would take Oliver Twist as an apprentice*.

3 ∾ OLIVER NEARLY BECOMES A CHIMNEY-SWEEP

Oliver was kept locked up, alone in a dark room, for a week. He cried all day. At night he put his hands over his eyes to shut out the dark. He crouched in the corner and tried to sleep.

Every morning Mr Bumble took him out into the yard. As Oliver washed himself at the pump*, Mr Bumble hit him with his cane.

Every day he was carried into the dining hall. There the beadle flogged* him in front of all the other boys.

One morning soon after, a chimney-sweep* called Mr Gamfield saw the notice on the workhouse gate. He went in and asked to speak to the board.

'This here boy, sir,' he said, 'might be just the boy I'm looking for. I need an apprentice.'

'Chimney-sweeping is a nasty trade,' said Mr Limbkins.

'Yes,' said another member of the board, 'boys have been smothered* in chimneys before now.'

The board knew that three or four boys who worked for Mr Gamfield had died up chimneys.

'We cannot accept your offer, Mr Gamfield,' said Mr Limbkins.

'Come, gentlemen,' said the sweep, 'don't be hard on a poor

man. What if I was to take the boy off your hands for less than a fiver?'

The board considered* this offer.

'Very well,' said Mr Limbkins. 'Three pounds ten. Not a farthing* more.'

'Is that all?' said Mr Gamfield.

'Take him, you silly fellow!' said the gentleman in the white waistcoat. 'He's just the boy for you. You'll have to beat him, now and again, but that will do him good. And his food won't cost you much. He hasn't been overfed since he was born.'

That afternoon Mr Bumble took Oliver to the magistrate*. 'You're going to be an apprentice, Oliver,' he told him. 'It will set you up for life, and make a man of you. Three pounds ten, that's what you've cost the parish! Three pounds ten, and all for an orphan that nobody loves.'

Mr Bumble told Oliver that the magistrate had to sign a special paper. 'Then the parish can wash its hands of you. You'll belong to Gamfield the sweep then.'

Mr Bumble led Oliver into the magistrate's office. The magistrate was sitting at a high desk. On one side of the desk stood Mr Limbkins, on the other, Mr Gamfield.

'Is this the boy?' asked the magistrate.

'Yes, your worship,' replied the beadle, 'this is him.'

'And is he fond of chimney-sweeping?'

'Very, your worship. He dotes on* it.'

The magistrate looked at Mr Gamfield. 'And you, sir – you will be his master? Will you treat him well, and feed him?'

'I will, sir,' said the sweep.

The magistrate looked down at the paper on his desk. He picked up his pen and was about to sign the paper. At that moment, he looked up and saw Oliver's pale, terrified face. He put down his pen. 'My boy, what is the matter?'

Oliver burst into tears.

'Stand away from him, Beadle,' said the magistrate. 'Let him come forward. Tell us what's the matter, and don't be afraid.'

Oliver fell on his knees. He begged to be sent back into that dark room, starved, flogged, killed even – anything rather be sent away with Mr Gamfield.

'Well I never!' cried Mr Bumble.

'Hold your tongue, Beadle,' said the magistrate. 'I will not sign these papers. This boy will not be apprentice to this sweep. Take him back to the workhouse, and see he's treated kindly.'

When the gentleman in the white waistcoat heard what had happened he said, 'I knew it! That boy will be hung, and drawn, and quartered*.'

The next day a new notice was pasted to the workhouse gates: 'Five Pounds and A Boy'.

4 ∾ OLIVER IS TAKEN ON BY MR SOWERBERRY, THE UNDERTAKER

Mr Bumble was standing by the gate when Mr Sowerberry, the undertaker*, came along. Mr Sowerberry looked at the notice. Mr Bumble tapped the notice with his cane. 'Generous terms*, Mr Sowerberry, generous terms.'

'It so happens that I'm looking for a house-boy*, Mr Bumble. Bring him along to my shop this evening. Then I can look him over.'

As Mr Bumble marched the boy to the undertaker's shop Oliver broke down and wept. 'What's the matter with you, you ungrateful boy?' bellowed* the beadle. 'Stop that blubbering* at once, or I'll beat you.'

'No, no, no, sir,' sobbed Oliver. 'I'll be good. Indeed I will, sir.'

'What's the matter, boy?'

'I'm so lonely, sir! So very lonely! Everybody hates me. Please, sir, don't be cross with me.'

The beadle looked at the helpless boy in astonishment. For a

moment his heart was touched with pity. He told Oliver to dry his eyes. Then he took the boy's hand and they walked on in silence.

When they arrived at the shop the undertaker had just put up the shutters*.

'Here I am, Mr Sowerberry,' said the beadle, 'and I've brought the boy.'

Oliver made a bow.

'So this is the boy, is it?' said Mr Sowerberry. He lifted his candle to get a better view of Oliver.

Just then Mrs Sowerberry came into the shop. 'Is this the boy?' she said. 'Dear me! He's very small.'

'But he'll grow, Mrs Sowerberry – he'll grow,' said Mr Bumble.

'I dare say he will,' she replied, 'on our food and drink! Come with me, you little bag of bones.'

Mrs Sowerberry took Oliver downstairs, into the kitchen under the shop.

A girl was sitting by the fire. 'Charlotte,' said Mrs Sowerberry, 'give this boy some of the bits that were put by for the dog.'

When Oliver had eaten the scraps of bread and meat, Mrs Sowerberry took him back upstairs. 'Your bed's under the counter. You don't mind sleeping with the coffins, I suppose.' Then she left him, taking the candle with her.

5 ∾ OLIVER MEETS MR NOAH CLAYPOLE

Oliver was terrified. There was an unfinished coffin in the middle of the shop. Oliver expected a frightful face to rear up from it at any moment. The shop was close* and hot. The air had the stale smell of death. The bed under the counter looked like a grave.

He was alone in a strange place – a boy with no one to care for, and no one to care for him. He was so unhappy, he wished his life

could end. He wished the bed was a grave. He wanted to lie down and sleep forever, with the tall grass waving about his head and the church bell soothing him to sleep.

Oliver was woken the next morning by a loud kicking on the shop door. It was Noah Claypole. Oliver unlocked the door and let him in.

'I suppose you're the new boy?' said Noah.

'Yes, sir.'

'How old are you?'

'Ten, sir.'

'I'm Mr Noah Claypole, and you're under me*.' He kicked Oliver hard. 'Now take down the shutters, you idle young ruffian*!'

Noah was a charity-boy*, but not an orphan. His parents lived nearby. His mother was a washerwoman* and his father a drunken soldier. The other shop-boys in the street called Noah 'Charity' and other cruel names.

Noah looked at Oliver. He was the lowest of the low – a workhouse orphan. Now Noah had someone to pick on.

When Mr and Mrs Sowerberry arrived at the shop they sent Oliver downstairs to get his breakfast. Noah and Charlotte were sitting by the fire. The girl gave Oliver some scraps of food. 'Sit over there, on that box,' she said, 'and hurry up. They'll want you to mind the shop.'

When Oliver had been working at the shop for some three months, Mr Sowerberry said to his wife, 'I'd like to speak to you about young Twist, my dear. He's a nice looking boy, is he not?'

'He should be. He eats enough,' she replied.

'I think he would make a delightful mute*, my love. Not for adult funerals, but for children's.'

The next morning Mr Bumble came to the shop. He handed a small scrap of paper to the undertaker.

'Aha!' said Mr Sowerberry brightly, 'an order for a coffin, eh? I'll see to it right away. Noah, look after the shop. Oliver, you come with me.'

Oliver followed Mr Sowerberry through the crowded streets. They came at last to a filthy, dark passageway. At the end of the passage was a door. Mr Sowerberry knocked. A young girl opened the door and they went in.

There was no fire in the room. A man was sitting next to the empty grate*. The man's face was very thin and pale. His eyes were bloodshot. Next to him was an old woman. There were some ragged children in the other corner. On the floor, under an old blanket, was the corpse.

Mr Sowerberry took out his tape and measured the body.

Suddenly, the man cried out, 'Nobody shall go near her! Keep away from her, damn you!'

'Nonsense, my good man,' said Mr Sowerberry.

'I tell you – I won't have her put in the ground.'

He burst into tears. The terrified children wept too. Mr Sowerberry hurried away, with Oliver hard on his heels*.

The next day Oliver returned to the house with Mr Sowerberry. Mr Bumble was there and four men from the workhouse. The coffin was carried to a shabby corner of the graveyard, where nettles grew.

After the brief service, Oliver and Mr Sowerberry walked back to the shop.

'Well, Oliver,' said the undertaker, 'how do you like it?'

'Not very much, sir,' replied Oliver.

'You'll get used to it in time, my boy.'

6 ✎ OLIVER ATTACKS NOAH CLAYPOLE

One day Noah and Oliver were in the kitchen as usual, having their dinner. Noah put his feet up on the table. He threw the bone he'd been chewing at Oliver and said, 'Where's your mother?'

'She's dead. And don't you say anything about her to me!'

'What did she die of?'

'A broken heart. That's what one of the old nurses told me.' Then he added, in a whisper, 'I think I know what it must be like to die of that.' He started to cry.

'What's set you off crying?'

'Not you. And don't you dare say anything more about her!'

'Your mother was wicked. It's a good thing she died in the workhouse, or else she'd have been sent to jail. Or hung, more like.'

In a blind fury, Oliver jumped up and grabbed Noah by the throat. He shook him until his teeth chattered. Then he knocked him to the ground with one mighty blow. Noah Claypole's cruel insult had set his blood on fire.

'He'll murder me!' squealed Noah. 'Help! Oliver's gone mad!'

Charlotte and Mrs Sowerberry came running down the stairs. Oliver was dragged, kicking and screaming, into the coal cellar*.

'What's to be done?' cried Mrs Sowerberry. 'The master is not at home.'

'Shall I send for the police, ma'am*?' said Charlotte.

'No. Noah, you must run to Mr Bumble. Tell him to come right away.'

7 ∾ OLIVER DEFENDS HIS MOTHER'S NAME

Noah Claypole ran all the way to the workhouse. He saw Mr Bumble standing by the gate. He was talking to the gentleman with the white waistcoat.

'Oh, Mr Bumble, sir!' said Noah. 'Oliver has—'

'What? He hasn't run away, has he?'

'No, sir. He turned vicious. He tried to murder me.'

'By Jove! I knew this would happen!' said the gentleman in the white waistcoat.

'And please, sir,' said Noah, 'Mrs Sowerberry wants to know if Mr Bumble can spare the time to come by the shop and flog him.'

'Certainly,' said the gentleman. 'You're a good boy. A very good boy. Here's a penny for you. Bumble, go with this boy straight away.'

The beadle went down to the cellar. Oliver was kicking on the door.

'Let me out!' he screamed.

'Oliver,' said Mr Bumble, 'do you know this here voice?'

'Yes.'

'And are you afraid of it? Do you tremble when I speak?'

'No.'

Mr Bumble was shocked. He looked at the others in stunned silence.

'Mr Bumble, he must be mad,' said Mrs Sowerberry.

'It's not madness, ma'am,' replied the beadle. 'It's meat.'

'What?' exclaimed Mrs Sowerberry.

'Meat, ma'am, meat. You've overfed him. If you'd kept the boy on gruel, this would never have happened.'

Just then Mr Sowerberry returned. When he heard what had happened he dragged Oliver out of the cellar. 'Why did you attack Noah?' he said.

'He called my mother names,' cried Oliver. 'He said she was wicked.'

'She was! And worse,' snapped Mrs Sowerberry.

'She wasn't!' shouted Oliver. 'That's a lie!'

Mrs Sowerberry burst into floods of tears. Mr Sowerberry beat Oliver, then shut him up in the back kitchen.

The next morning, before it was fully light, Oliver wrapped what few possessions he had in a handkerchief and left the shop. He walked quickly through the empty streets. The road took him past the workhouse. There was no one around, just one small child working in the garden. Oliver recognized him.

'Dick,' he said, 'is anyone up?'

'Nobody but me.'

'You mustn't say you saw me, Dick. I'm running away. They beat me and ill-use me. But how pale you look!'

'I heard the doctor say that I'm dying. I'm glad to see you. But you must not stop.'

'I shall see you again, Dick. I know I shall. You will be well and happy.'

'I hope so – after I am dead, but not before. I know the doctor must be right. I dream about heaven and angels, and kind faces that I never see when I'm awake. Goodbye and God bless you, Oliver.'

8 ∾ OLIVER WALKS TO LONDON AND MEETS FAGIN AND HIS BOYS

It was eight o'clock now and he was five miles from the town. He sat down to rest by a milestone*. The stone told him he was seventy miles from London. London! Nobody would find him there, not even Mr Bumble.

He opened his bundle. He had a crust of bread, a shirt, two pairs of socks and a penny.

He walked twenty miles that day. He tasted nothing but the crust of dry bread, and some water he begged along the way. When night came, he lay down under a haystack and tried to sleep. He was frightened and hungry, and more alone than he had ever been.

When he woke the next morning he was cold and stiff. His feet were sore. He was so weak his legs trembled as he walked. As he passed through some villages he saw large painted signs: 'Persons found begging in this parish will be sent to jail'. He moved on as quickly as he could. A turnpike-keeper* took pity on him. He gave him a meal of bread and cheese.

Early on the seventh day Oliver limped into the little town of Barnet*. He sat down upon a cold doorstep to rest his bleeding feet. A boy came up to him and said, 'Hallo, what's the matter?'

The boy was about the same age as Oliver. He had a dirty face, with a snub nose* and sharp, ugly eyes. He was wearing a man's coat that reached down to his heels. He walked with a swagger*, as if he owned the street. He sat down on the step, next to Oliver.

'What's the matter?' he asked again.

'I'm tired and hungry,' said Oliver, beginning to cry.

'Going to London?'

'Yes.'

'Got any lodgings*?'

'No.'

'Money?'

'No.'

'So I suppose you want some place to sleep tonight, don't you?'

'I do indeed. I haven't slept under a roof since—'

'Don't fret*. I know a respectable old gentleman who lives in London. He'll give you lodgings for nothing. My name's Jack Dawkins – but my friends call me the Artful Dodger. What's yours?'

'Oliver, Oliver Twist.'

'Well, Oliver, we'd best be going, if we are to get to London by nightfall.'

It was dark when they reached the old gentleman's house. The Dodger led Oliver into a back room. The walls and ceilings were black with age and dirt. There were several rough beds made of old sacks. Four or five boys, none older than the Dodger, were sitting around smoking clay pipes and drinking gin. Behind them was a line, over which a great number of silk handkerchiefs were hanging.

Next to the fire there was an old man. He was cooking sausages in a frying pan. He had an evil, repulsive* face. It was half-hidden by his long, matted red hair.

'This is my new friend, Fagin,' said the Dodger. 'His name's Oliver Twist.'

Fagin grinned. He made a low bow, then took Oliver by the hand. 'We are very glad to see you, Oliver – very,' he said. 'Dodger, take off the sausages and pull a box up to the fire for Oliver.'

Oliver sat down in front of the fire. He ate supper with the other boys. Fagin gave him a mug of hot water and gin. He was very tired. He felt himself being gently lifted onto one of the sacks. Soon he was fast asleep.

9 ∾ OLIVER AND FAGIN PLAY A GAME

It was very late next morning when Oliver awoke from his deep sleep. There was no one else in the room, except Fagin. He was sitting by the fire, boiling up coffee in a pan. As Oliver lay there, half asleep, half awake, the old man got up. He went to a dark corner of the room and opened a little trapdoor in the floor. He took out a small box and put it on the table. He sat down and opened the box. He took out a magnificent gold watch, sparkling with jewels. 'Aha!' he said to himself. 'Clever boys. Clever boys.'

He put the watch back. Then he took out half a dozen more, as well as rings and bracelets. It seemed to Oliver that the little box was bursting with priceless treasures. Fagin was staring at the jewels, but he had a far-away look in his eye. 'Five of them. Poor lads. Hung by the neck. But none of them said a word about old

Fagin. What a fine thing capital punishment* is. Dead men can't speak.'

When Fagin looked up and saw Oliver watching him he cried out, 'What's this! Why are you awake? What have you seen? Speak out, boy.'

'I couldn't sleep any longer, sir.'

Fagin closed the box and put it back in its hiding place under the floor.

'Did you see my pretty things, my dear?'

'Yes, sir,' said Oliver.

'They are mine, my dear. All I have to live on in my old age.'

Oliver got up. A little while later, the Dodger and another boy called Charley Bates came in. The four sat down to breakfast.

'Well,' said Fagin to the Dodger, 'I hope you've been hard at work this morning.' The old man gave Oliver a sly look. The Dodger laughed.

Charley Bates said, 'We've been working very hard, Fagin.'

The boys put a pile of wallets and handkerchiefs on the table. Fagin looked at them closely.

'Very good, Charley. Very good, Dodger.'

After breakfast was cleared away Fagin said, 'Would you like to make pocket-handkerchiefs as easy as Charley and Dodger, Oliver?'

'Very much indeed,' replied Oliver, 'if you'll teach me.'

'He's so green*,' Charley said to the Dodger. The Dodger laughed.

'Come, my dears,' said Fagin, 'let's show Oliver our little game.'

Fagin filled the pockets of his long ragged coat with handkerchiefs and wallets. He walked up and down the room, like a gentleman looking in shop windows.

The Dodger and Charley followed him. The game was simple. The boys had to take the wallets and handkerchiefs from Fagin's pocket without him noticing. Charley and the Dodger were very good at the game.

Then two young ladies called to see Charley and Dodger. One was called Bet, the other Nancy. They drank some gin. The old man gave Charley and the Dodger some spending money. Then they went out with the young women.

When they were alone, Fagin smiled at Oliver. 'Is my handkerchief hanging out of my pocket?' he said.

'Yes, sir.'

'See if you can take it, just like Dodger.'

The old man turned his back. Oliver gently pulled out the handkerchief.

'Is it gone?' asked Fagin.

'Here it is, sir.'

'You're a clever boy, my dear.' He patted Oliver on the head. 'I never saw a sharper lad. Here's a shilling* for you!'

10 ∾ OLIVER DISCOVERS THE TRUTH
ABOUT FAGIN'S BOYS

It was many days before Oliver left Fagin's room. Every morning he unpicked the initials on dozens of silk handkerchiefs. He played the handkerchief game with Fagin and the other boys.

Then, one bright morning, Fagin said he could go out with Charley and the Dodger. They walked through the narrow crowded streets until they came to a quiet square. The Dodger pointed to an old gentleman standing outside a bookshop, reading a book. 'He'll do, Charley,' said Dodger. 'Oliver, you stay here.'

The two boys walked slowly across the square. The Dodger tiptoed up to the old gentleman. He slipped his hand in the old man's pocket and pulled out a handkerchief. He passed the handkerchief to Charley. Then both boys ran off at top speed.

Oliver was horrified. Now he understood the real purpose of Fagin's 'game'. He was confused and frightened. Without thinking, he ran after the Dodger and Charley.

At that moment the old gentleman put his hand in his pocket. His handkerchief was gone! He turned around and saw Oliver. 'Stop thief!' he shouted, and ran after the boy.

'Stop thief! Stop that boy!' The cry was taken up by a hundred voices. The shouts echoed along the narrow streets. Within seconds there was an angry crowd chasing Oliver.

Oliver ran for his life. He turned a corner and came face to face with a tall, well-built man. The man punched him in the face. Oliver fell to the pavement. The crowd gathered round. The old gentleman arrived, out of breath. 'Stand aside,' he said. 'Give him air.'

Oliver lay in the mud and dust. His mouth was bleeding.

A police officer arrived. He grabbed Oliver by the collar. 'Come on, get up!' he said sharply.

'It wasn't me, sir,' said Oliver. 'It was two other boys.'

The policeman pulled Oliver to his feet. 'What other boys? I don't see no other boys.'

'Don't hurt him, constable,' said the old gentleman.

The policeman grabbed hold of Oliver's jacket. 'Come with me, you little devil.'

'Where are you taking him?' asked the old gentleman.

'To the magistrate, sir. And you'd better come along too.'

11 ∾ OLIVER MEETS MR FANG,
        THE MAGISTRATE

Oliver was locked in a police cell in the yard behind the magistrate's office. The cell was cold, dark and dirty. The old gentleman stood by as the policeman turned the key in the lock.

'There is something in that boy's face,' the old man said to himself. 'Where have I seen that face before?' But no matter how hard he tried, he could not remember.

Mr Fang, the magistrate, was a tall, lean* man. He had a stern*, red face. When Oliver was led into his office, Mr Fang looked up with an angry scowl*. 'Is this the boy? What has he done?' said Mr Fang, crossly.

'May I explain, sir?' said the old gentleman, with a bow.

'Who are you?' snapped Mr Fang.

'My name is Brownlow,' replied the old gentleman. 'I was standing outside the bookshop when my handkerchief was stolen.'

'Stolen? By this young scoundrel*?'

'I'm not – I don't think—' stammered Mr Brownlow. 'When the boy was caught, he was searched. Nothing was found.' He looked at Oliver. The boy was trembling. His face was white with

26

terror. 'I don't think this boy is a thief,' said Mr Brownlow. 'I think this boy is very ill.'

'Nonsense!' snapped the magistrate. 'What's your name, boy?'

Oliver raised his head. He tried to speak, but could not. The room started to spin. Oliver fainted.

'Thinks he can pull the wool over my eyes, does he?' said Fang. 'I'll teach him a lesson he won't forget. Three months hard labour*. Next case!'

Two men were about to carry Oliver back to his cell when an elderly man dressed in black ran into the office.

'Stop! For Heaven's sake, stop. I saw it all. I am the owner of the bookstall. I saw three boys. The other two ran off. This boy is innocent.'

'Why didn't you speak sooner?' growled the magistrate.

'There was no one to mind the shop. I had to wait for help. I ran all the way.'

The magistrate gave Oliver a long hard look, as if to say, 'If I had my way, you scoundrel, I'd have you hung.'

'Case dismissed!' he said, at last. 'Clear the office!'

Oliver was carried out. He lay on his back on the pavement. His face was a deathly white.

'Poor boy, poor boy,' said Mr Brownlow, bending over him. 'Call a coach, somebody. Quickly.'

12 ∾ OLIVER IS CARED FOR BY MR BROWNLOW

The coach took Oliver and Mr Brownlow to a neat house in a quiet, shady street. Oliver was put to bed. When he awoke, after a long and fitful* sleep, he saw an old lady sitting by his bed.

'What room is this? Where am I?' Oliver asked, weakly.

'Hush, my dear,' said the old lady softly. 'You have been very bad – as bad as can be. Lie still, there's a dear. The doctor will be here shortly.'

The doctor smiled at Oliver. 'Well now, you are a great deal better! Give him a little tea, Mrs Bedwin, and some dry toast. I shall come by again tomorrow.'

Mrs Bedwin looked after him just as a mother would. Three days later Oliver was strong enough to get out of bed. He was still too weak to walk. He was carried downstairs to Mrs Bedwin's parlour.

Oliver noticed a painting in the parlour. It hung above the fireplace. It was the portrait of a young woman. He asked Mrs Bedwin, 'Who is that lady, ma'am?'

'I don't know, my dear.'

'She's very pretty. But her eyes are so sorrowful. And they seem to follow me. Her face makes my heart beat. It's as if she knew me. As if she wants to speak to me, but cannot.'

'Lord save us!' said Mrs Bedwin. 'Don't talk that way, child. You're weak and feverish* after your illness.'

Later that day Mr Brownlow came to Mrs Bedwin's room. 'How do you feel?' he asked, sitting down next to Oliver.

'Very happy, sir,' replied the boy.

'And what is your name?'

'Oliver Twist, sir.'

'That's a strange name.'

The old gentleman stared at Oliver. He felt sure he had seen the boy's face before. It reminded him of someone. But who?

Then suddenly he knew. 'Look! Look there, Mrs Bedwin!' He pointed to the portrait above the fireplace. 'And now – look here.' He pointed to Oliver. 'See – the same mouth, the same eyes, every feature the same!'

This exclamation* startled Oliver, and he fell back in a faint.

13 ❧ FAGIN HEARS ABOUT OLIVER'S ARREST

The Dodger and Charley Bates had hidden under a low dark archway until the crowd chasing Oliver had passed. Then they made their way back to Fagin's room.

'What's this!' shouted Fagin. 'Where's the boy?' He grabbed the Dodger by the collar. 'Speak, damn you, or I'll throttle* you.'

'The police have got him,' cried the Dodger. 'Now let me go, will you.'

Just then the door opened and a thick-set* man of about thirty-five came into the room. With him was a young woman. A scraggy white dog followed at their heels.

'What are you up to? Ill-treating your boys again?' growled the man in a deep voice. 'It's a wonder they don't murder you. I would, if I was them. I'd have done it years ago.'

The man was dressed in a very dirty black velvet jacket. He was unshaven and had dark staring eyes. He called to his scraggy dog. 'Get over there! Lie down!' He kicked the dog and sent it rolling across the floor. It lay down in the corner without a sound.

Fagin let go of the Dodger and grinned at the man. 'Bill Sikes – well, well. And Nancy. What brings you here?'

'Get me some gin, Fagin,' said Sikes.

Bill Sikes and Nancy sat down at the table. Fagin gave them some gin. He told them how Oliver had been arrested. 'If the boy talks,' said the old man, 'then we're in trouble, Bill.'

'True enough,' said Sikes. 'Then somebody should go to the police station and find out what's happened to the boy.'

'But who?' said Fagin nervously. 'It wouldn't be safe for me – or you, Bill.'

'Nancy,' said Sikes. 'You'll go, won't you, my dear.' There was

such a cold threat in Bill Sikes' voice that Nancy knew it would be dangerous to say no.

So Nancy went to the police cells behind the magistrate's office.

'Have you seen my little brother?' she asked, weeping. 'Is there a little boy here?'

A policeman told her what had happened – how the old gentleman had taken him away in a coach.

As soon as Nancy told Bill what she had heard he left Fagin's room without saying another word.

'We must find out where he is!' cried Fagin. 'He must be found.' He opened a drawer and took out some coins. 'Here's money – Dodger, Charley. And you too, Nancy – you did well, my dear. We must leave this place tonight. It's not safe here any more. You know where to find me.'

'What do we do if we find the boy? Do we kidnap him and take him to the other house?' asked Dodger.

'Yes,' said Fagin, 'and if he means to blab* about us to his new friends, then we may have to kill him!'

14 ∾ OLIVER TALKS TO MR BROWNLOW

When Oliver was next carried down to Mrs Bedwin's parlour he saw that the portrait had been taken down. 'Why have they taken her away?' he asked.

'Mr Brownlow's orders, my dear,' said the old lady. 'It seemed to upset you. It might stop you getting well.'

'Oh, no. It didn't upset me. I liked to see it.'

'Then as soon as you are well we will put the picture back. That's a promise. Now Mr Brownlow has asked to see you. He's in the library, downstairs.'

Oliver had never seen so many books. The room was lined

with books, from floor to ceiling. 'A great many books, are there not, Oliver?' said Mr Brownlow.

'Indeed, sir. A great number. I never saw so many.'

'Would you like to grow up a clever man, and write books?'

'I think I would rather read them, sir.'

Mr Brownlow laughed. 'Come, sit here next to me. I have something I must tell you.'

'You're not going to send me away!' cried Oliver, alarmed. 'Please don't send me back to that wretched* place!'

'My dear child,' said the old gentleman, 'I shall never send you away – unless you give me cause*. Come now. Dry your eyes. You say you're an orphan, without a friend in the world. Let me hear your story. Speak the truth.'

Oliver began his story. He was telling the old gentleman about the workhouse, and Mr Bumble the beadle, when a visitor arrived. It was Mr Brownlow's old friend, Mr Grimwig.

'Hallo! What have we here?' said Mr Grimwig, looking at Oliver.

'This is young Oliver Twist,' said Mr Brownlow, 'the boy we were speaking about.'

Oliver bowed.

'How are you, boy?' said Mr Grimwig.

'A great deal better, thank you, sir.'

'And when are we going to hear the full and true adventures of Oliver Twist?' asked Grimwig.

'Not today,' interrupted Mr Brownlow. 'I would rather he was alone with me at the time. Now, Oliver, I want you to do something for me. I want you to take these books to the bookshop. Can you do that?'

'Yes, sir! I'll run all the way.'

'I owe the shopkeeper some money. Take this five-pound note. Mrs Bedwin will give you directions.'

Mr Brownlow and Mr Grimwig sat down by the fire. Mr Brownlow took out his pocket watch and put it on the table. 'Let me see – he should be back in twenty minutes, at the latest.'

'Do you really think he's going to come back?' said Mr Grimwig.

'Don't you?'

'I do not!'

'Why not?'

'He's wearing a new suit of clothes. He carrying a valuable set of books. He's got a five-pound note in his pocket. That's why not!'

It grew dark. The two gentlemen sat, in silence, with the watch between them.

Bill Sikes met Fagin in the gloomy back room of a filthy beer-house. 'What are you going to do, Bill?' asked the old man nervously.

'Don't you mean, what are we going to do?' snarled Sikes. 'If I go down*, so will you, Fagin. We're in this together. Have you brought my share of the money?'

Fagin handed Sikes a small brown-paper packet.

Just then Nancy came into the dingy* back room. 'Well, Nancy, have you been on the scent*?'

'Yes, I have, Bill,' she said, sitting down. 'And dog tired I am too. The boy Oliver's been ill. At death's door, I hear. Tucked up in bed.'

Later that same day, Oliver was on his way to the bookshop. He turned a corner into a narrow lane and was startled by a young woman who called out, 'Oh, my dear brother! I've found you at last.'

Oliver wanted to run away, but the young woman threw her arms around him and held him tight.

'Let me go!' cried Oliver.

Two women were passing nearby. They came over to see what was the matter.

'This is my brother,' said the young woman. 'He ran away a month ago. Broke his mother's heart. Joined a band of thieves, he did.'

'You young ruffian!' said one woman.

'Go home, you little brute!' cried the other.

Oliver struggled to get free. He caught a glimpse of the young woman's face.

'Why, it's Nancy!' he said.

'You see, he knows me,' said Nancy.

The door of a nearby beer-house opened and a man lurched out into the lane. There was a scraggy white dog snapping at his heels. 'What the devil is this?' said the man. 'Oliver, come home to your mother, you young dog.'

'I don't belong to them. I don't know them. Help! Help!' cried the boy. He struggled to escape the man's powerful grip. The man grabbed Oliver by the collar. 'Come on, you young villain! Here, Bull's-eye – mind him, boy! Mind him!'

Weak with illness, terrified by the growling dog and its brutal* owner, what could Oliver do? He was dragged away into the gloomy maze of narrow stinking streets.

It was dark now. The streetlamps were lit. Mrs Bedwin was waiting by the front door. The servant had been sent out twenty times to look for Oliver. In the library the two old gentlemen sat in the dark, with the watch between them.

Bill and Nancy led Oliver away from the crowded streets into a narrow lane. Bill stopped and shouted to his dog, 'Bull's-eye! Come here!'

The dog looked up at his master and growled. 'See this here boy, Bull's-eye? If he speaks – just one word – rip his throat out!' The dog licked his lips and snarled.

They walked on, through dark and dirty lanes, for almost an hour. Then Sikes stopped at a door and knocked softly. The door opened and Oliver was pushed inside. Oliver heard the door bolted and barred* behind him. Then he heard the Dodger's voice. 'Fagin's upstairs, Bill.'

A flight of narrow wooden stairs led to a low evil-smelling room. Inside it were Fagin and Charley Bates.

'Here's Oliver,' said Charley. 'Look at his new clothes. And his books. Proper little gentleman, aren't you, Oliver?'

'Delighted to see you looking so well, my dear,' said Fagin. 'Why didn't you write and let me know you were coming? I would have got something special for your supper.'

Charley and Dodger laughed. The Dodger slipped his hand into Oliver's pocket and pulled out the five-pound note.

'That's mine!' cried Sikes. 'Give it here, Dodger.'

'No, Bill, fair's fair – it's mine.'

'You can have the books.'

When he heard this, Oliver fell on his knees at Fagin's feet. 'No! They belong to the old gentleman. He took me into his house. He nursed me. I was near dying of the fever. Please, send back the books and the money. Keep me here all my life, if you must. But send the books and money back. He'll think I am a thief. Please, have mercy on me!'

Sikes looked at Fagin and laughed. 'The boy's right, Fagin.

The dear old gentleman will think he's a thief. He won't come looking for him, will he?'

Fagin looked at Oliver and grinned. 'No, Bill. You're right. He won't come looking for poor Oliver, because if he finds him he'll have to take him to the magistrate. And the dear old gentleman is too soft-hearted to do that.'

When he heard this, Oliver ran out of the door and down the stairs.

'Keep hold of the dog, Bill!' cried Nancy. She stood between Bill and the door. 'Keep him back. He'll tear the boy to pieces.'

'Get out of my way,' snarled Sikes, 'or I'll split your skull against the wall.'

'I don't care. I don't care. That child won't be torn down by the dog, unless you kill me first.'

The Dodger and Charley caught Oliver at the foot of the

stairs. They dragged him back into the room. Fagin picked up a heavy stick. 'So you wanted to run away, did you, Oliver? Wanted to get help? Wanted to call the police?'

The old man hit Oliver on the back with the stick.

Nancy rushed at Fagin, grabbed the stick, and threw it in the fire.

'What's got into her?' cried Fagin.

'The girl's gone mad!' replied Sikes, savagely.

'No, she hasn't!' said Nancy. 'Don't think that, Fagin.'

'Then keep quiet,' said Fagin.

'I won't do that, neither,' replied Nancy. 'I won't stand by and see this done! You've got the boy. What more do you want?'

Nancy made a rush at Fagin, but Sikes stepped forward and grabbed her. Nancy tried to fight, but his strong hands held her wrists, until she fainted. 'She's got a worse temper than Bull's-eye,' said Bill, and he lay Nancy down on a sack in the corner.

Oliver was taken next door, to a grimy kitchen. 'You can sleep here,' said the Dodger. 'Take your smart clothes off. Fagin will look after them for you.'

Oliver lay down on the filthy mattress. Sick and weary, he cried himself to sleep, as he had done so many times before.

17 ❧ MR BUMBLE GOES TO LONDON

Mr Bumble, the beadle, left the workhouse early in the morning. He was on his way to London, on 'parish business'. First he had to call on Mrs Mann, who looked after the parish orphans.

'Good morning, ma'am. How are the children today?'

'They're all as well as can be expected, Mr Bumble,' said Mrs Mann. 'Except the two that died last week. And little Dick.'

'Isn't that boy better? Where is he? Bring him here, ma'am.'

The boy, Dick, was sent for. He stood before the beadle,

trembling, not daring to lift his eyes from the floor. He was pale and thin. His limbs were wasted away, like those of an old man.

'What's the matter with you, Dick?' thundered Mr Bumble.

'I would like— ' stammered the child.

Mr Bumble was clearly shocked. 'What!'

'I would like a piece of paper. And someone who can write words down for me. And they could keep it for me, when I am in the grave.'

'What do you mean, boy?' asked the beadle.

'I want my friend Oliver Twist to know I didn't forget him. I want him to know how often I cried thinking about him, all alone, with no one to help him.'

Mr Bumble looked at Mrs Mann in astonishment. 'What a hard-faced little wretch, ma'am. Take him away!'

The orphan, Dick, was led away. Mrs Mann said to the beadle, 'Sir, I hope you don't blame me. It isn't my fault that—'

'No, ma'am,' said Mr Bumble, shaking his head, 'I blame Oliver Twist!'

Mr Bumble arrived in London the next day. He took a room in the inn* where the coach stopped. That night, after a hearty* supper, he sat by the fire reading the newspaper. He was astonished to read this advertisement on the front page:

FIVE POUNDS REWARD
A young boy, named Oliver Twist, ran away or was kidnapped, last Thursday. A reward of five pounds will be given to anyone who has information about the boy.

Mr Bumble, wide-eyed, read the advertisement several times. It also gave a full description of Oliver, and Mr Brownlow's address.

Without delay, the beadle made his way to Mr Brownlow's house. The old gentleman was at home. His friend, Mr Grimwig, was with him. Mrs Bedwin took Mr Bumble into the library. 'Mr Brownlow, sir!' she said, breathlessly. 'Here's a Mr Bumble, with news of our dear little Oliver!'

'You've seen the advertisement?' said the old gentleman.

'Yes, sir,' replied the beadle.

'Do you know where this poor boy is now?'

'No, sir.'

'What do you know of him?'

Mr Bumble sat down and started to tell all he knew about Oliver Twist. He was an orphan, a parish boy, with low* and vicious parents. He was an ungrateful, wicked boy. A violent boy who attacked poor Noah Claypole, and ran away from kind Mr Sowerberry who was teaching him an honest trade.

'I knew it,' said Mr Grimwig smugly, 'the boy is a villain.'

Mr Brownlow paced the room to and fro. He was very upset. Mr Bumble, five pounds richer for his information, said goodnight and left.

Mrs Bedwin burst into tears. 'This can't be right, sir,' she sobbed. 'I can't believe it. He was a dear, gentle child. I know what children are, sir. I have done, these last forty years. Oliver is a—'

'Mrs Bedwin!' said the old gentleman crossly, 'I never want to hear the boy's name again. Is that clear? Never!'

18 ❧ OLIVER MEETS MR TOM CHITLING

About noon the next day, the Dodger and Charley went out. Fagin told Oliver that if he spoke to the police, they would all hang – Bill, Nancy, Fagin, the boys – and Oliver. Little Oliver's blood ran cold. 'But if you keep quiet,' said the old man, patting him on the head, 'then we'll be very good friends, my dear. Very good friends indeed.' With that, he went out, locking the room door behind him.

Oliver was locked in the room, from early morning until midnight, every day for a week. After that Fagin left the door unlocked, and Oliver was free to wander about the house.

It was a very dirty place, black with dust and neglect*. The windows had heavy wooden shutters. The rooms were gloomy and filled with strange, menacing* shadows.

One day Charley and the Dodger came back early from their thieving. The Dodger sat on the table, smoking a pipe, swinging his legs. 'Why don't you want to work for Fagin, Oliver?' he said.

'I don't want to,' said the boy, timidly. 'I wish they would let me go. I – I – I would rather go.'

'And Fagin would rather you stay!' laughed Charley.

'Look here!' said the Dodger. He took a fistful of coins from his pocket. 'And there's plenty more where that came from. This is the life, isn't it, Charley?'

Charley nodded. 'If you come in with Fagin and the rest of us, we'll make something of you.'

Just then Fagin came back, with a young man whom Oliver had not seen before.

'This is our… friend, Mr Tom Chitling, Oliver,' said Fagin. 'He's… been away, haven't you, Tom?' Tom laughed.

'Would you like a glass of gin, Tom?' said the old man.

'Forty-two days without a drop – what do you think! Give me the bottle.'

'Where do you think Mr Chitling has been for the last six weeks, Oliver?' asked Fagin with a wicked grin.

'I – I – I don't know, sir,' stammered Oliver.

Charley, the Dodger and Fagin laughed. Tom Chitling gave Oliver a strange look, then said coldly, 'You'll find your way there soon enough, you mark my words.'

From that day on, Oliver was seldom* left alone. He played the old game with Fagin and the boys every day. Fagin told them

stories of the robberies he'd done when he was younger. He was a great story-teller. Oliver found himself laughing with the others at the old man's tales. He had been so sad, so lonely. Now, at last, it seemed that he'd found some friends.

19 ◞ FAGIN AND BILL SIKES PLAN A ROBBERY

It was a damp, windy night. A black mist hung over the town. Fagin made his way through the maze of dirty streets to Bill Sikes' house.

'Now, Bill,' said the old man, sitting down before the fire, 'when are you going to do that robbery at Chertsey? I can't wait to get my hands on all that silver plate.'

'It can't be done,' said Sikes.

'Can't be done? Why?'

'Not as an inside job. Toby Crackit's tried to get someone on the inside, but he's had no luck.'

'That's a sad thing, my dear. We'd set our heart on that silver.'

'We could do it as an outside job,' said Sikes, 'but I'd want another fifty pounds for that. For the risk.'

'Of course,' said Fagin.

'And I need a boy. He mustn't be a big one.'

'Oliver!' said Fagin. 'He's the boy for you, my dear. It's time he started working for his bread. The others are too big.'

'Well, he's just the size we want,' said Bill.

'And he'll do everything he's told – if you frighten him enough. Once he's done a job, once he's been thieving, then he's ours for life!'

'Ours!' said Sikes. 'Yours, you mean.'

'When will you do the job?'

'Tomorrow night. Bring the boy here tomorrow. Then hold your tongue and keep the melting-pot* ready. That's all you have to do, Fagin.'

Fagin made his way back to his hideout. Dodger was sitting up, waiting for his return. 'Where's Oliver? I want to speak to him,' said the old man.

'In bed, an hour ago,' replied Dodger.

Fagin opened the kitchen door. The boy was lying, fast asleep, on a bed of sacks on the floor. His face was pale with worry and sadness.

'Not now,' said Fagin, turning softly away. 'Tomorrow. Tomorrow.'

20 ∾ OLIVER IS TAKEN TO BILL SIKES' HOUSE

When Oliver awoke he was surprised to find a new pair of shoes, with thick soles, next to his bed. Fagin gave the boy some breakfast. 'You've got to go to Bill Sikes' house tonight, my dear,' said the old man.

'To – to – stop there, sir?' asked Oliver, anxiously.

'No, we wouldn't send you away, my dear. That would be cruel. Don't be afraid, Oliver, you shall be coming back to us. But mind you do as Bill tells you. He's a rough man when his blood's up*.'

Fagin said no more about it all day, but that night he put a candle on the table for Oliver.

'Here's a book for you to read, till they come to fetch you. Good night.'

'Good night,' replied Oliver, softly.

Oliver opened the book. It was a history of the lives of great criminals. The pages were dirty with use. The terrible crimes made his blood run cold. He shut the book and fell to his knees and prayed.

Oliver was alone in the kitchen when Nancy came for him. She closed the door behind her. 'Are you ready, Oliver?' she said, quietly.

'Am I to go with you?' asked Oliver.

Nancy nodded. 'Yes, I've come from Bill.'

'Why does Bill want me?'

Nancy put her finger to her lips and pointed to the door. 'Hush,' she whispered, drawing him close. 'I know you want to get away from here. But this is not the time. I saved you from a beating once before. And I will again. You must be quiet and do as you are told.' She showed Oliver some terrible bruises on her arms and neck. 'Remember these! Every word from you is a blow for me. Come now. Give me your hand. We must go.'

When they got to Sikes' house Bill said, 'Did he come quietly, Nancy?'

'Like a lamb,' replied the young woman.

Bill sat himself down at the table and stood the boy in front of him. There was a pistol on the table. Bill picked it up. 'Do you know what this is?'

Oliver nodded. The robber grabbed his wrist tightly. He pressed the gun against the boy's head. 'One word, and I'll blow your brains out. Do you hear me?'

After supper Sikes threw himself down on the bed and told Nancy to wake him at five. Oliver lay down in his clothes on a mattress on the floor. It was a long time before he fell asleep.

When he woke it was still dark. The rain was beating on the window panes. The sky was black and cloudy. 'Now then, look sharp!' growled Sikes. 'Or you'll get no breakfast.'

Oliver was too sick with fear to eat much. So a few minutes later Bill said farewell to Nancy and led Oliver out into the dark streets.

21 ∾ OLIVER AND BILL ON THE ROAD

They walked all day, through the busy markets and crowded streets of the city. At nightfall they came to an inn called the

Coach and Horses. They went inside and ordered some supper by the kitchen fire. After they had eaten Bill seemed in no hurry to move on. He sat by the fire and smoked his pipe.

Oliver, tired out from the day's march, fell asleep. He woke up when he heard Bill Sikes say, 'Are you going to Shepperton*?'

He was talking to a man who had come into the inn while Oliver had been asleep.

'I am,' said the man. 'The wagon's in the yard. Is it a lift you're wanting?'

'Yes,' said Sikes. 'My boy, Ned – we've been on the road all day – he's dead on his feet.'

'Then I'm your man,' said the driver. 'Come on. We'd best be on our way, if we're to get there by midnight. The old horse needs her beauty sleep too.'

Two miles past Shepperton the wagon stopped. Bill got down. He took the boy by the hand and set off walking once more. They were on a lonely country road. Far away Oliver could see the lights of a town.

After a while they came to a bridge. Oliver looked down into the dark swirling water. Fear gripped the boy. 'The river!' thought Oliver. 'He's brought me here to drown me.' He was about to struggle for his life when he saw that he was standing in front of an old tumbledown* house. Sikes grabbed him by the arm and together they went into the ghostly ruin.

22 ∾ OLIVER TAKES PART IN A ROBBERY

'Hallo!' cried a loud voice, as soon as they entered the ruin.

'Don't make such a noise, Toby,' said Bill. 'Bring a light. Where's Barney?'

'Here, Bill,' said another voice from the darkness. 'Come in. Come in.'

Sikes pushed Oliver down the dark passage. They entered a low dark room, with a smoky fire and a few sticks of broken furniture. Toby Crackit and Barney were sitting by the fire. 'Is this the boy?' said Toby.

'Yes. He's one of Fagin's.'

Oliver sat down in the corner, by the fire. His head was aching. He had no idea where he was, or what was happening. But now he was exhausted and past caring. Soon he was fast asleep.

At half past one the next morning Toby Crackit woke him up, saying, 'Time to go to work, young fellow.' Sikes and Crackit left the house, with Oliver between them. Barney was left on guard.

Soon they arrived at the town of Chertsey*. They heard a church bell strike two. They came, at last, to a large house, surrounded by a high wall. Toby climbed to the top of the wall and pulled Oliver up behind him. Soon all three were lying on the grass at the other side.

Now, for the first time, Oliver realized what was happening. It was not murder they had in mind, but robbery! A wave of terror washed over him. He felt his legs buckle* under him. He fell to his knees.

'Get up!' growled Sikes. He pulled out his pistol. 'Or I'll spread your brains all over the grass.'

Toby pulled Oliver to his feet and half-dragged him towards the back of the house. Sikes pointed to a small window. 'I'm going to put you in there. Open the front door, and let us in.'

Sikes took a crow-bar* from under his cloak and prised* open the window. Then he put Oliver through the window, feet first. Once the boy was inside Sikes said, 'Take this lamp. Can you see the stairs? Then go up them to the front door.'

Sikes still had hold of Oliver's collar. But Oliver had made up his mind. As soon as the robber let go, he would run up the stairs and wake the family.

Suddenly there was a noise in the hall. 'Back! Back!' cried Sikes, pulling on Oliver's collar.

A light appeared. Then two half-dressed men, at the top of the stairs. A flash. A loud noise. Smoke. A crash. And Oliver staggered back.

Bill fired his pistol at the two men. They ran away. He dragged the boy through the window. 'Give me a scarf!' he shouted to Toby. 'They've hit him. Quick! See how he bleeds!'

Then Oliver heard the loud ringing of bells, gun-fire, shouts. He felt himself being carried at a rapid pace. Then a cold deathly feeling crept over him, and he saw or heard no more.

23 ∾ MR BUMBLE TAKES TEA WITH MRS CORNEY

The night was bitterly cold. Snow lay thick on the ground. Mrs Corney, the matron* of the workhouse where Oliver was born, was sitting before a cheerful fire in her parlour. There was a soft tap on the door. It was Mr Bumble. He shook the snow off his coat and sat down by the fire.

'Hard weather, Mr Bumble,' said Mrs Corney.

'Hard, indeed, ma'am.'

'Will you take some tea, Mr Bumble?'

'Indeed, ma'am. Thank you.'

'Sweet, Mr Bumble?' asked the matron, taking up the sugar bowl.

'Very sweet indeed,' replied the beadle, squeezing Mrs Corney's hand.

Mr Bumble moved his chair a little closer to the matron. Mrs Corney was a widow. Mr Bumble wanted to marry her. He leaned over and put his arm round her waist. He kissed her on the cheek.

'Mr Bumble,' she whispered, 'I shall scream.'

Just then there was a loud rapping on the parlour door. It was Martha, one of the old women from the workhouse. 'Come quickly, mistress,' she said. 'It's old Sally. She's going fast.'

'What's that to me?' said Mrs Corney crossly. 'I can't keep her alive, can I?'

'She says she's got something to tell you, mistress – something you must hear.'

24 ∾ OLD SALLY'S STORY

Old Sally was asleep when Mrs Corney came to her bedside in the bare workhouse attic*. Mrs Corney sat down by the fire. Martha sat by the bed.

After a while, Sally cried out, 'Who's there?'

The matron went to the bedside. 'What is it?' she said impatiently. 'What have you got to tell me? Out with it!'

'Send her away,' said the old woman. 'Send Martha away. What I have to say is for your ears only.'

Mrs Corney pushed Martha out of the room and closed the door.

'Now, listen to me,' said the dying woman. 'In this very room – in this very bed – I nursed a young woman. She gave birth to a baby boy. I robbed her. I stole the only thing she had. It was gold. They would have treated him better, if they'd known.'

'Treated who better?' asked the matron. 'Known what? Speak up, woman!'

'The boy grew up to be just like his mother. I could see her face in his.'

'Which boy?'

'They called him Oliver,' said the old woman, feebly. 'The gold I stole was—'

'Yes, yes – what?' cried the matron.

But old Sally did not speak another word. As Mrs Corney left the room Martha asked, 'What did she say, mistress?'

'Nothing,' said the matron, sharply. 'Nothing at all.'

25 ∾ FAGIN LEARNS THAT THE ROBBERY HAS GONE WRONG

While old Sally was dying in the workhouse, Fagin was sitting by the fire in his hideout. The Dodger, Charley, and Tom Chitling were there too. The three young thieves were playing cards. They were laughing and joking, but Fagin was staring into the flames, deep in thought. Then he got to his feet and paced up and down the gloomy room.

It was nearly midnight when they heard a knock at the street door.

The Dodger went down to see who it was. It was Toby Crackit.

'Where's Bill and the boy?' cried Fagin. 'Where are they?'

'The robbery went wrong,' said Toby.

'I know,' replied Fagin, pulling a newspaper from his pocket. 'Where's Bill? And the boy?'

'The boy was hit. We cut across the fields, dragging the boy between us. Through hedges and ditches. Damn! The whole country was awake, and the dogs upon us.'

'The boy!'

'Bill had him on his back. He was running like the wind. Then he stopped to get his breath. The boy was cold, Fagin. Stone cold. The dogs were nearly on us. It was every man for himself – or the gallows*. We left the boy in the ditch – alive or dead. That's all I know.'

Fagin did not stop to hear more. He ran from the room, down the stairs and out of the house.

Fagin walked as fast as he could through the by-ways* and alleys. He went by way of Snow Hill and Holborn Hill. From there he went to Saffron Hill. The narrow lane was lined with second-hand shops. The shops were piled high with silk handkerchiefs. This was where Fagin sold his stolen goods.

He came, at last, to the Three Cripples inn. The inn was crowded with noisy drunks. A girl was singing. The landlord came over to Fagin. 'What can I do for you, Mr Fagin?'

'Is he here?' said Fagin, in a whisper.

'Monks, do you mean?'

'Hush!' said Fagin, looking over his shoulder.

'He's not here yet. I expected him an hour ago. Will you wait, Mr Fagin?'

'No! Tell him I came. Tell him he must come to see me tonight.'

Fagin left the inn without another word. He went straight away to Bill Sikes' house. Nancy was there, alone. She was drunk. She was sitting at the table, with her head on her arms. Fagin told her Toby Crackit's story. Nancy listened, unmoved*.

'Where do you think Bill is now, my dear?' asked Fagin.

Nancy did not reply. She hid her face from Fagin. She was sobbing. Suddenly she looked up at him and cried, 'The boy's better off dead than living with thieves like us, Fagin. No harm can come to him now.'

When he heard this Fagin flew into a rage. 'That boy's worth hundreds of pounds to me! Now all that's been thrown away because—'

He stopped suddenly. He looked down at the girl. She was crying. Fagin sat down. He was trembling. What a fool he had been to blurt out his secret like that. Had Nancy heard him?

The old man stood up. He went over to Nancy and put his hand on her shoulder.

'Nancy, my dear,' he said gently. 'Did you hear what I said just now? About the boy?'

'I hope he's dead, and out of harm's way,' she sobbed.

Fagin, reassured that Nancy had not heard, left the house and made his way back to his hideout.

Fagin was fumbling for his door-key when a dark figure stepped out of the shadows nearby. 'Ah, Monks,' said the old man.

'Where the devil have you been, Fagin?'

'On business,' replied Fagin. 'Your business. Come in, quickly. We must talk.'

Fagin made sure that Toby and the boys were asleep. He took Monks into one of the empty upper rooms. They sat down, the flickering candle between them on the dusty floor. Fagin told Monks about the robbery and how it had gone wrong.

Monks was angry. 'You should have kept the boy here with you. I never wanted him dead, Fagin. I wanted you to train him, like the others. In twelve months, he'd be a proper thief. Then you could turn him in. He'd be sent to the prison colony* in Australia, and that would be the end of it.'

'You know what happened when Oliver went out with the Dodger and Charley!' said Fagin. 'I wasn't going to let that happen again.'

'That wasn't my fault,' said Monks.

'But if that hadn't happened you would never have seen Oliver. You would never have known that he was the very boy you were looking for all these years.'

'Who's that?' said Monks suddenly, pointing to the shuttered window.

'There's no one here,' said Fagin.

'I saw the shadow of a woman, in a cloak and bonnet*!'

'It was just your imagination.'

'I swear I saw it.' Monks was shaking. 'There's someone here.'

They looked in all the rooms. They were bare, cold and empty – all as still as death itself.

27 ∾ MR BUMBLE'S QUESTION

Mr Bumble was sitting by the fire, dozing. Mrs Corney hurried into the parlour and sat down next to him. 'What is it, ma'am?' said the beadle. 'You look quite out of sorts*. Will you have a little gin in your tea?'

Mrs Corney said she would, 'But just a little, Mr Bumble. To keep out the cold.'

'This is a very comfortable parlour, Mrs Corney,' said the beadle. 'And, if I may be so bold, you are a very comfortable woman.'

The matron blushed. Mr Bumble kissed her. 'You know that Mr Slout, the master of this workhouse, is dying?'

'Indeed, I do. Poor man.'

'The doctor says he won't live more than a week. Then there will be a vacancy*. A vacancy that must be filled.' Mr Bumble put his arm around the matron's waist. 'If I were master of this workhouse, would you marry me?'

'Why, yes, Mr Bumble. As soon as ever you please!'

28 ∾ OLIVER MEETS MISS ROSE MAYLIE

Bill Sikes stopped to get his breath. The body of the wounded boy lay across his knee. Sikes could hear men's voices and the sound of dogs barking.

'Crackit, wait!' cried the robber. 'Help me with the boy.'

Toby ran back and helped Bill lay the boy in the ditch. 'It's no use, Bill,' he said. 'Look there! They're on to us.'

Two men were climbing the gate into the field where the robbers stood.

Sikes paused for a second, then threw his cloak over Oliver, and ran like a fox before the hounds.

When Oliver awoke the sky was growing light. He was in great pain. His left arm hung heavy and useless at his side. The scarf that bound* it was soaked in blood. He knew that if he lay there he would surely die. He staggered to his feet. He was dizzy, like a drunken man. He stumbled across the field towards the gate. He came, at last, to a house. It looked familiar. It was the very house they had tried to rob! He knocked on the front door, then fell down in a faint on the step.

The door was opened by Mr Giles, the butler*. He was one of the men who had chased Bill, Oliver, and Toby the night before. 'It's one of the thieves!' cried Mr Giles. 'Wounded! I shot him. Quick, Brittles, bring a light.'

Brittles, a servant at the house, brought a lantern*. Between them they lifted Oliver into the hallway. Just then, a young woman appeared at the head of the stairs. 'What is it, Giles?' she whispered.

'One of the thieves, Miss Rose. Badly wounded.'

'Stay there. And don't make any more noise. You'll frighten my aunt more than the robbers did. Wait there, while I go and speak with her.'

Miss Rose Maylie returned a moment later. 'Take the boy up to your room, Giles. Brittles – saddle a pony, and go and fetch the police and the doctor. Be quick now!'

29 ∾ DOCTOR LOSBERNE ARRIVES

Doctor Losberne arrived two hours later. Miss Rose Maylie and her aunt, Mrs Maylie, were having breakfast. 'I never heard of such a thing!' said the doctor. 'Bless my soul. I never heard of such a thing, Mrs Maylie. You might have been murdered in your bed, dear lady. Dear me. So unexpected! And in the dead of night too. And you, Miss Rose, are you all right?'

'Quite all right,' said the young woman, 'but the poor boy upstairs is not. It is him you have been called to see.'

Miss Rose Maylie was not yet seventeen. She was slim, with a kind, gentle face and deep blue eyes.

The doctor turned to the butler. 'Then show me the way, Giles. I'll look in again on my way down, Mrs Maylie.'

The doctor was gone a long time. When he came back into the breakfast room, he closed the door and stood with his back to it, as if to keep it shut. He spoke in a very mysterious way. 'This is a strange business,' he said, shaking his head. 'Quite extraordinary. Have you seen this thief, Mrs Maylie?'

'No,' answered the old lady.

'Or heard anything about him?'

'No. But what do you mean, sir – "This is a strange business"?'

'I think you should come and see the thief, right away. You too, Miss Rose.'

30 ∾ OLIVER TELLS HIS LIFE STORY

The doctor drew back the bed-curtain. There lay a child. His face was worn with pain and exhaustion*. He was fast asleep. Miss Rose sat down beside the bed. She brushed Oliver's hair from his face. As she did so, her tears fell upon his forehead.

Oliver stirred*, and smiled in his sleep.

'What can this mean?' exclaimed the elderly lady. 'This poor child is no robber.'

'Look how young he is,' said Miss Rose. 'I don't think he has ever known a mother's love. He has been ill-used, I'm sure of it. Aunt, dear aunt – prison is no place for this sick child.'

Mrs Maylie smiled. 'My dear, I could never harm a single hair

on this child's head.' The elderly lady turned to Doctor Losberne. 'What can I do to save him, sir?'

'Let me think, ma'am,' said the doctor, 'let me think.'

Later Oliver was well enough to tell them all his simple history. His pillow was smoothed by gentle hands that night. Love and kindness watched over him as he slept. He was calm and happy, and could have died without a murmur.

The doctor went downstairs to find Mr Giles, the butler. 'I've sent for the police, sir. How is the patient*?' asked Giles.

'So-so,' replied the doctor. 'I'm afraid you are in a spot of trouble, Giles. If that boy dies…'

'I didn't mean to kill him, sir.'

'And can you be sure he was the boy at the window last night? It was dark. All that gunsmoke and alarm! A man could easily make a mistake, Giles. A very bad mistake.'

At that moment there was a loud knock on the door. Two policemen, Blathers and Duff, were let in. The doctor met them in the hallway. 'This is the lady of the house – Mrs Maylie,' said the doctor.

'And where is the boy?' said Blathers.

'Ah, yes, the boy,' said Doctor Losberne. 'One of the servants found the boy at the front door. Saw the boy had been shot. Put two and two together and made five. Thought the boy had something to do with the break-in, but it's nonsense.'

'Well, we'll soon sniff out the truth, sir,' said Duff. 'Who is this boy? Where did he come from? He didn't drop out of the clouds, did he, sir?'

'Of course not,' replied the doctor. 'I know his whole history. We can talk about that presently*. But first you will want to see the window where the thieves made their attempt.'

'Very good, sir,' said Blathers. 'Then we must talk to the boy.'

Oliver had been dozing, but he looked worse. Dr Losberne stood by the bed.

'The boy told me the whole story. He was trespassing* in some woods nearby. He's not sure where. Somebody shot at him. He doesn't know who. Probably a gamekeeper*. Thought the boy was a poacher*. He made his way to this house, and passed out on the doorstep. Then Giles grabbed him—'

'I thought it was the boy, sir,' said the butler to the policemen.

'What boy?' said Duff.

'The housebreakers'* boy,' said Giles.

'Well, do you still think this is the boy?' said Blathers.

Giles shook his head. 'I don't know. I couldn't say for certain. I don't think it's the boy. I'm almost certain that it isn't.'

To add to the muddle and confusion, Brittles said the same

thing. He could not swear that Oliver was the boy he had seen at the window. Some time later the two policemen left Mrs Maylie's house, satisfied that Oliver had not taken part in the crime.

32 ∾ OLIVER GOES TO LIVE IN THE COUNTRY

Oliver was very ill. The bullet had smashed a bone in his arm. Lying in the cold wet ditch had given him a high fever. It was many weeks before he started to get better.

When at last he did recover, Rose told him, 'We are going to stay at our cottage in the country. My aunt says you must come with us, Oliver. It's very quiet there, and the fresh air will do you good. Would you like that?'

'Indeed, yes. Thank you, ma'am. But—'

'What is it? What's troubling you?'

'The kind gentleman, Mr Brownlow, who took care of me. I would like him to know I am safe and being cared for.'

'Do you have his address?'

'Yes, ma'am.'

'You are still too poorly to travel. When you are better, Doctor Losberne will take you to see Mr Brownlow.'

But Mr Brownlow had sold his house. He had gone to the West Indies to live. Oliver was very disappointed. He had wanted the old gentleman to know the truth.

A fortnight later Mrs Maylie, Rose, and Oliver left the big house at Chertsey and went to stay at the cottage. Oliver was very happy there. He went for long walks in the woods and fields, by himself or with Miss Rose. Every morning Oliver went to visit an old white-haired man who lived near the church. The kind old man helped Oliver with his reading and writing. In the evenings Rose would play the piano and sing for him.

Three months slipped by. During this time the old lady and her niece* grew to love Oliver, and Oliver grew to love them.

33 ❧ MISS ROSE IS VERY ILL

One day, Oliver came back from his morning walk and saw Mrs Maylie sitting in the garden. She was crying. 'Oh, Oliver,' she said quietly, 'Rose was taken ill last night. This morning she is worse, much worse.'

'Will she – die?' asked Oliver.

The old lady did not answer.

'She must not die!' cried Oliver. 'Heaven will not let her die so young.'

'Hush!' said Mrs Maylie, laying her hand on Oliver's head. 'Come now, dry your eyes. I've written to Doctor Losberne. I want you to take this letter to the George inn and give it to the post-boy* there. If you hurry it will go on the midday coach.'

It was four miles across the fields to the George inn. Oliver ran like the wind. He gave the letter to the post-boy and started back straight away. As he was hurrying out of the inn he ran into a tall man standing at the door.

'I beg your pardon, sir,' said Oliver. 'I was in a hurry to get home and didn't see you.'

The man stared at him as if he had seen a ghost. 'What the devil is this?' he cried. He grabbed the boy by the arm. 'He was dead. Dead. Now he's come back from the grave!'

Oliver thought the man must be drunk. He struggled to get free.

'What are you doing here? You're dead,' snarled the man. He shook his fist in the boy's face, then fell to the ground in a fit.

Oliver ran off, as fast as his legs would carry him.

Doctor Losberne arrived the following evening. For two long days Rose was at death's door. There was nothing anyone could do but wait. Then, on the morning of the third day, the doctor came into the parlour.

'What of Rose?' cried the old lady.

'Be calm, ma'am, and pray.'

'She is dead! Let me go to her!'

'No!' cried the doctor. 'The worst is past. She will live to bless us all for years to come.'

34 ❧ MR HARRY MAYLIE ARRIVES

It was almost too much happiness to bear. Oliver went for a walk to think, and to pick flowers for Rose. As he was walking back, a carriage came along at great speed. It stopped. Inside were Giles and another man, a stranger.

'This is Mr Harry Maylie, Oliver,' said Giles.

'What news of Miss Rose, Oliver?' asked Harry.

'Much better, sir.'

'Are you sure?'

'Yes, sir. I heard the doctor say she would bless us all for many years to come.'

With that, the carriage clattered on towards the house.

Mrs Maylie met her son at the door. 'Mother,' he said, 'why didn't you write to me earlier? You know how I feel about Rose. I could never have forgiven you if she had died and I had not been at her side.'

'My dear son,' said the old lady quietly, 'I know how you feel about Rose. And you know how I feel about your wish to marry her. It is not as simple as you would like. You know the difficulties you will face – and you know the reasons. Rose knows them too. Now I must go to her.'

'Will you tell her I am here?'

'Of course.'

Oliver had a little room on the ground floor, at the back of the cottage. It looked out into the garden. One evening Oliver was sitting by the window, reading. It was very warm and Oliver fell asleep. He had a dream. In his dream he heard Fagin's voice saying, 'That's him, sure enough. Bill Sikes thought he was dead. But that's him. That's Oliver Twist.' And another voice replied, 'Are you sure?'

Oliver woke from the dream with a start*. There – there at the window, so close he could have touched him, was Fagin! And beside him the man he'd seen at the inn. Oliver cried out in terror, and in a flash both men were gone.

Giles and Harry heard Oliver's cries. 'It was Fagin!' said the boy shaking with fear. 'He was here – and another man.'

'Which way did they go?' said Harry.

'Across the field.'

'Then they can't be far away. Come on, Giles. You too, Oliver.'

They searched the fields and woods all around the cottage, but there was no sign of Fagin and the other man.

'Perhaps it was a dream, Oliver,' said Harry.

'No, indeed, sir. I saw them as plainly as I see you now.'

'And who was the other man?'

'The same man I told you about – the man at the inn.'

The following day Harry and Oliver walked over to the George inn. Nobody there knew anything about Fagin's mysterious companion.

Rose was now well enough to leave her room and take short walks in the garden.

One morning Harry found her there, alone. 'I must talk to you, Rose. You know how I feel about you. I have loved you for years. I want you to marry me.'

Rose shook her head. 'Harry,' she said gently, 'we can never marry. We can be the best of friends, but never more than that. You have great talent and ambition. You are going to be an important man in public life. The people you will mix with would look down on me because of my family. There is a stain on my name*. If I married you, your enemies would use it against you. I do not want to bring shame and failure on you – on the son of the lady who has been like a mother to me.'

'So you do not love me?'

'I love you too much. That is why we cannot marry.'

The following morning Oliver was sorry to hear that Harry Maylie was going back to London. Before he climbed into the coach with Doctor Losberne, Harry said quietly, 'Will you write to me, Oliver?'

'Yes, sir.'

'I want you to tell me how my mother and Miss Rose are. Tell me what walks you take and what you talk about. But don't mention this to them, Oliver. Let it be a secret between you and me. Mind you tell me everything. I depend on you.'

With that, Mr Harry Maylie jumped into the doctor's coach. Rose watched the coach disappear down the dusty lane, tears in her sad blue eyes.

Mr Bumble had married Mrs Corney and was now master of the workhouse. Their marriage, just two months old, was not a happy one. 'Are you going to sit there by the fire all day, snoring?' said Mrs Bumble.

'I'll sit here as long as I like,' said Mr Bumble.

But the master's wife had other ideas. She grabbed him by the throat and slapped his bald head. 'Get up! Get out! You fat, lazy lump!' she cried. 'And take yourself away from here, before I do something desperate.'

Mr Bumble had never been so miserable. Two months before he had been the parish beadle, a respected man. He left the workhouse and walked along the street to the public house. The back parlour was empty. Bumble ordered gin and sat down by the fire, feeling very sorry for himself. A tall dark man, wearing a long cloak, came into the parlour. He sat down next to Mr Bumble. 'You were the beadle here once, were you not?'

'I was,' replied Bumble.

'What are you now?'

'Master of the workhouse.'

'I want some information from you.' He placed two gold coins on the table. Bumble slipped them into his pocket.

'Twelve years ago last winter, a boy was born in the workhouse,' said the man.

'A great many boys are born there.'

I am speaking of one particular boy – a meek*, pale-faced boy. He was apprenticed to the coffin-maker, Sowerberry. How I wish that boy was dead. If only he'd made his own coffin and buried himself in it!'

'You mean Oliver Twist. I remember him.'

'It's not him I'm interested in. Let's have no more of him! The old woman who nursed his mother, where is she?'

'She died last winter,' replied Mr Bumble, 'but before she died she spoke to another woman about the boy Twist.'

'How can I find this other woman?'

'Only through me.'

'When?'

'Tomorrow,' said Bumble.

'Very well,' said the stranger. 'Meet me at nine in the evening, at this address.' He gave Mr Bumble a scrap of paper.

'What name shall I ask for?' said Mr Bumble.

'Monks!' said the stranger.

38 ∾ MR AND MRS BUMBLE DO BUSINESS WITH MONKS

Mr and Mrs Bumble turned off the main street of the town into a steep narrow lane that led down to the river. They came to an old ramshackle* warehouse* on the river bank. Mr Bumble looked at the address on the scrap of paper. 'This must be the place.'

'Up here!' cried a voice from above. It was Monks at a second-storey window. 'Come up, but be careful where you walk. The timbers* are rotten.'

Soon all three were seated in a dimly lit room. 'Now, let us get down to business,' said Monks. 'What did the old woman, Sally, tell you?'

'First,' said Mrs Bumble, 'what's it worth?'

'It may be worth nothing. It may be worth twenty pounds.'

'Twenty pounds,' said the matron, 'and I'll tell you all I know.'

Monks put the money on the table.

'When old Sally died, she and I were alone.'

'Are you sure?'

'I stood by the body when death came over it.'

'Go on.'

'Sally told me that she'd robbed Twist's mother.'

'What? What did she take?'

'This,' said Mrs Bumble, putting a little gold locket* on the table. 'There are two locks of hair and a gold wedding ring inside it. And the name "Agnes" was engraved* on the inside.'

Monks snatched up the locket. 'Is this all?'

'That's all. Is this what you wanted?'

'It is.'

'Can this ever be used against me?' said Mrs Bumble.

'Never!' cried Monks. 'See here.' He got to his feet and pulled open a large trapdoor in the dusty wooden floor. 'Look,' he said.

Mr and Mrs Bumble looked down at the dark swirling river.

'If you dropped a man's body down there, where would it be tomorrow morning?' said Monks.

'Twelve miles down the river, and cut to pieces,' replied Bumble.

With that, Monks threw the locket into the racing tide. 'The sea gives up its dead. But it keeps its gold and silver to itself.' He turned to the workhouse master and his wife. 'Forget the name Monks. Forget we ever met. Now, get away from here as fast as you can!'

39 ∾ NANCY MAKES A BRAVE DECISION

Bill Sikes was more dead than alive. He lay on his bed, wrapped in an old coat. His dog sat by the bedside, growling at every noise that came up from the street below. 'What time is it, Nancy?' the robber asked.

70

'Not long past seven,' replied the girl. 'How do you feel tonight, Bill?'

'Weak as water! Here, lend me a hand to get up. Where's Fagin?'

Just then Fagin came in. 'Where've you been, Fagin? I might have been dead ten times over! What do you mean, leaving me in this state for three weeks and more?' cried Bill.

'I've been away from London, my dear, on business.'

'You left me here to rot!'

'Don't get in a temper, Bill. I never forgot you. Not once.'

'If it hadn't been for Nancy, I might have died. Have you got any money? I need some money tonight.'

'Not with me, Bill. I never carry cash, you know that. It's all back at the hideout.'

'I need it tonight!'

'Then let Nancy come back with me for it. You trust Nancy, don't you, Bill?'

When Nancy and Fagin arrived at the hideout Monks was waiting on the stairs.

'Go up, Nancy,' said the old man. 'I have some business with this gentleman. I'll only be a minute.' Nancy went on up the steep stairs. She stopped on the dark landing to listen to what the two men were saying.

'When did you get back?' said Fagin.

'Two hours ago.'

'Did you see him?'

'Yes.'

Nancy heard everything that was said. As Monks left the house, she slipped into the kitchen. 'Hurry up, Fagin,' she said as the old man came upstairs. 'Where's Bill's money? He'll be in a foul temper if you keep him waiting much longer.'

When Nancy left Fagin's hideout she sat down on a doorstep.

She was confused, and unsure what to do next. Suddenly, she stood up and hurried off down the narrow street. Not towards Bill Sikes' house, but in the opposite direction – towards the west end of London.

40 ∾ NANCY MEETS ROSE MAYLIE

Within the hour, Nancy was in a hotel room in a quiet street near Hyde Park.

Across the table from her sat Miss Rose Maylie.

'Is that door locked?' said Nancy nervously.

'Yes,' said Rose. 'Why?'

'Because what I am about to tell you will put my life and the lives of others in great danger. I'm the girl that dragged little Oliver back to Fagin's den.'

'You!'

'They'll murder me if they find out I've been here. Do you know a man called Monks?'

'No.'

'He knows you. He knew you were here, in this very hotel. That's how I was able to find you. I heard him and Fagin talking. He saw Oliver, by chance, in the street. He recognized him. Said he'd been looking for him. I don't know why. Then last night, this man Monks turns up again. I heard Monks say, "So now the only proof of the boy's identity* lies at the bottom of the river." He called Oliver his brother.'

'His brother!' cried Rose.

'His very words, miss. Then he spoke of you and another young lady. He said you would pay thousands of pounds to know who Oliver really is.'

Rose was shocked. After a moment's thought she said quietly, 'Until I get to bottom of this mystery you must stay here, with me.'

'No!' said Nancy. 'I must go back. If I told others – the police – what I've told you, then Bill Sikes would surely hang. I'll not have his death on my hands.'

'But how shall I find you again?'

'Do you promise to keep my secret?'

'I promise.'

'Every Sunday night, between eleven and midnight, you will find me on London Bridge – if I am alive.'

41 ∾ OLIVER MEETS MR BROWNLOW AGAIN

Oliver and Giles had gone to stay at the Hyde Park hotel with Rose. One morning Rose was about to write to Harry Maylie, when Oliver and Giles came running in. Oliver was out of breath and very agitated*.

'What is it?' asked Miss Rose. 'What's happened?'

'I saw him!' cried the boy. 'Mr Brownlow. We were out walking. I saw him. I'm sure it was him. Going into a house, nearby. I'm sure it was him.'

Rose turned to Giles. 'Quickly, Giles. Get a coach. If Oliver is right, then there's no time to lose.'

Fifteen minutes later Rose Maylie was sitting in Mr Brownlow's drawing-room*.

Mr Grimwig was there, and Mrs Bedwin. 'Some time ago you showed great kindness to a young friend of mine – a boy,' said Miss Maylie. 'I am sure you would like to know what has become of him.'

'Indeed!' said Mr Brownlow, shocked. 'May I ask his name?'

'Oliver Twist.'

'I knew it!' cried Mrs Bedwin. 'I knew he'd come back.'

Mr Brownlow drew his chair closer to Rose's. 'Oliver! What do you know about Oliver?'

Rose told them everything that had happened to Oliver since he had left Mr Brownlow's house. She also told them what Nancy had said the night before.

'Where is he now, my dear?' asked Mrs Bedwin.

'In the coach, outside.'

'Then bring him in!' cried the old gentleman.

Oliver ran into the room and, when he saw Mrs Bedwin, he threw his arms around her neck.

'God be praised,' she sobbed. 'He's back.'

After much hugging and hand-shaking and back-slapping, and a good few tears, Rose and Oliver left. Mr Brownlow promised to meet them again, at the hotel, at eight o'clock that evening.

Oliver had been sent to bed. Mrs Maylie was there to greet Mr Brownlow. So were Rose and Doctor Losberne. 'This is a muddle and a mystery,' said Mr Brownlow. 'It will be no easy matter

getting to the bottom of this, you mark my words. But we must, if we're to see this villain Monks behind bars.'

'We can't go to the police!' cried Rose. 'I promised the girl.'

'Then we will keep that promise,' said the old gentleman sternly. 'You cannot see her until next Sunday night. Today is Tuesday. In the mean time, we must say nothing. This matter must be kept secret – even from Oliver himself.'

42 ∿ MR AND MRS CLAYPOLE COME TO LONDON

On the same night that Nancy had met Rose Maylie, Noah Claypole and Charlotte – Mrs Sowerberry's servant – were making their way to London.

'Come on, can't you?' said Noah.

'Is it much farther? I'm dog-tired.'

'We're as good as there. Look, them's the lights of London.'

'There's a public house, Noah. Can we stop there for the night?'

'That would be a stupid thing to do, Charlotte. If Sowerberry comes after us, that's the first place he'd look. And you'd be taken back in handcuffs.'

'Don't put all the blame on me, Noah.'

'You took the money from the till.'

'I took it for you, Noah. I took it for you, my dear.'

They trudged on, making their way through the crowded streets, until – by chance – they came to the Three Cripples inn. Barney, Fagin's friend, was behind the bar, reading a grubby newspaper.

'We want a bed for the night, and some cold meat and beer,' said Noah.

Barney showed them into a small private back room.

When Fagin came into the inn a few minutes later, Barney said, 'Strangers in the back room, Fagin. Up from the country. Might be looking for work. Your sort of work – if you get my meaning.'

Fagin grinned. He put his finger to his lips. He crept down the passage that led to the small back room. He put his ear to the door.

'I'm going to be a gentleman,' said Noah. 'No more coffins. And you, Charlotte, shall be a gentleman's wife and live like a lady.'

'And what will we live on?' asked Charlotte. 'You can't expect to empty a till every day and get away with it.'

'Tills be blowed! There's pockets and purses and mail-coaches* and banks—'

Noah stopped as Fagin came into the room. The old man sat down at the next table. 'So, my dear,' he said with an evil grin, 'you like to empty tills.'

Noah's face went deathly pale. He almost fell off his chair.

'Ha, you're lucky is was only me that heard what you said. Don't worry, my dear. I'm in that kind of business myself, and so are the people who run this inn. The Three Cripples is the safest place in London for the likes of us. I can always find work for a sharp fellow like you. Come to my house at ten tomorrow. Barney will show you the way.'

Fagin stood up to leave. 'What's your name, my dear?'

'Mr Bolter,' replied Noah, 'Mr Morris Bolter. And this is Mrs Bolter.'

43 ∾ NOAH CLAYPOLE JOINS FAGIN'S BOYS

When Noah Claypole, alias* Morris Bolter, arrived at Fagin's hideout the next day the old man was in a foul mood.

'What's the matter?' said Noah.

'My best boy – the Dodger – the police nabbed* him yesterday. They caught him picking a pocket. He'll get life, nothing less. He's up before the magistrate this very morning. I want you to go down there, Mr Bolter my dear, and find out what's happened to the boy.'

Noah slipped into the back of the crowded courtroom.

'What is the next case?' bellowed the magistrate.

'A pickpocket, your worship,' answered a policeman.

'Has the boy been here before?'

'No – but he should have been! I know all about him, your worship. A police officer saw him steal a watch, and three silk handkerchiefs.'

The magistrate looked at the Dodger. 'Have you anything to say for yourself?'

'No,' said the Dodger.

'Take him down,' said the magistrate. 'Next case!'

Nancy was terrified that Bill or Fagin would find out about her meeting with Rose Maylie. As each day passed, she lived in fear of her life. She was pale and thin, silent and dejected*.

It was Sunday night. Fagin and Bill were discussing business. As the church clock struck eleven, Nancy put on her bonnet.

'Where are you going at this time of night?' asked Sikes.

'Not far,' said Nancy.

'Where are you going?'

'I said, not far.'

'Where?'

'I want a breath of air.'

'Then put your head out of that window.'

She went to the door. Bill grabbed her bonnet and threw it on the floor.

Nancy turned to Fagin. 'Tell him to let me go, Fagin. It'll be better for him. Do you hear me!' she screamed.

Sikes grabbed her arm. 'If you don't shut up, the dog will have you by the throat! What's going on here? What's come over you?'

She would not answer, so he locked her in the next room. 'I've never known her like this before, Fagin,' he said. 'Something's troubling her, that's a fact.'

As Fagin made his way home later that night something was troubling him too. Nancy was up to something, he was sure of that. She'd need to be watched. And Fagin knew just the person to do the watching.

45 ∽ FAGIN GIVES NOAH A JOB

'Bolter, my dear,' said Fagin, 'I have a job for you. It's a special job that requires great care and skill.'

'Then I'm your man.'

'I want you to follow a woman.'

'Who is she?'

'One of us, my dear.'

'And she's up to something, is she?'

'She's found some new friends, and I must know who they are.'

46 ⌇ NOAH FOLLOWS NANCY

Nancy met Miss Rose Maylie and Mr Brownlow the following Sunday on London Bridge. Mr Noah Claypole was hiding in the shadows nearby. He heard every word that was said.

'Why were you not here last Sunday?' asked the old gentleman.

'I couldn't come. It isn't easy for me to get away.'

'We must find this man Monks. Will you help us? What does he look like?'

'He's tall and dark – a strong man, with deep-set eyes. He's got a strange mark—'

Mr Brownlow cried out, 'A red mark? Like a burn? On his neck?'

'Yes!' said Nancy, shocked. 'You know this man?'

'I think I do. We shall see. You have been most helpful, young lady. Is there anything we can do for you?'

'Nothing,' said Nancy, turning to go. 'I am past all hope now. I have gone too far to turn back.'

'Wait. Please wait,' said Rose. 'Do you need money?'

Nancy shook her head sadly. 'I have not done this for money.' With that, she turned and melted away into the night.

47 ❧ BILL SIKES, MURDERER

As dawn broke, Fagin sat in his hideout in front of a dying fire. His face was so pale that he looked like a ghost just risen from the grave.

Noah Claypole lay at his feet, fast asleep on a filthy mattress.

He heard footsteps on the stairs. It was Bill Sikes.

Fagin shook Noah. 'Wake up, here's Bill.'

Noah sat up, rubbing his eyes.

'Poor lad,' said Fagin to Bill. 'He's tired. He's been up all night – watching her, Bill.'

'What do you mean?' said Sikes.

Fagin pulled Noah to his feet. 'Tell him. Tell Bill what you heard!'

'I followed her – to London Bridge. She met a young woman and a gentleman. She told them about you, Bill, and Mr Fagin. And a man called Monks.'

'Hell's fire!' cried Sikes. He rushed from the room.

'Bill! Bill!' Fagin called after him. 'Don't be too violent, Bill. Be careful.'

Nancy was lying on the bed, half dressed. 'Is that you, Bill?' she said sleepily.

'It's me,' said Sikes, bolting the door. He dragged her from the bed.

'Bill!' she cried. 'What's got into you?'

'You were watched tonight. You were followed, and every word you said was heard.'

'Then spare my life, Bill, because I saved yours.'

As Sikes' strong hands closed around her throat she struggled free. She ran to the door. Sikes picked up a heavy club and struck her dead.

48 ∾ BILL SIKES ON THE RUN

Bill Sikes put a rug over Nancy's body. He threw the club on the fire and burned it. Then he washed himself and rubbed his clothes to remove the spots of blood. There was blood all over the floor. Even the dog's paws were bloody.

He left the city as soon as he could. He walked here and there, through fields and farms. At noon, exhausted, he lay down under a hedge and slept. Bull's-eye curled up at his feet.

By nine o'clock in the evening he came to an inn. He ordered some bread and cheese and beer for himself, and some scraps for his dog. He sat down in a quiet corner. After he had eaten he fell asleep. He was startled from his sleep by two men talking.

'What's happening up in town, Ben?' said the first man.

'I heard talk of a murder,' said the second. 'Dreadful business. Young woman, beaten to death.'

'Any news of the killer?'

'They say he's run away to Birmingham. He'll not get far. They'll soon find him, and stretch his ugly neck.'

'Amen to that, Ben.'

Sikes spent that night hiding in a wood. At dawn the next day he decided to go back to London. 'Fagin will give me money,' he said to himself, 'and I'll take a boat to France.'

Sikes knew the police would be looking for him and his dog. He'd have to drown it. When they came to a deep pond, Sikes picked up a large stone and tied his handkerchief around it. 'Come here, Bull's-eye,' he called. The dog backed away, growling. 'Come here!' shouted Sikes. But the dog ran off down the lane, towards London.

Three strong men grabbed Monks and bundled him into a coach. They took him to Mr Brownlow's house. He was shown to a small back room where the old gentleman was waiting. 'Wait outside, gentlemen,' said Mr Brownlow. 'I must speak to this rogue* in private. Lock the door.'

'What is the meaning of this?' cried Monks. 'On whose orders was I kidnapped in the street?'

'On mine. You, sir, are guilty of robbery and fraud*. If you do not do exactly as I say I will call the police.'

'I didn't expect this – not from my father's oldest friend,' said Monks.

'It is because I was your father's oldest friend that I am trying to keep the police out of this, Edward Leeford.'

'What do you want with me?'

'You have a brother.'

'I have no brother. I was an only child.'

'You have a brother. When your parents separated your father met another woman. She had a child. This child was born in the workhouse. His mother died there. Of course, you know this, don't you, Edward? "The only proof of the boy's identity lies at the bottom of the river." I have a portrait of Oliver's mother. Your father gave it to me. When Oliver came to my house he seemed to recognize that face. Before I could find out Oliver's true identity was he was taken from me. I knew that you alone could solve the mystery. I discovered you had an estate* in the West Indies. I went there to look for you, but I was told you had returned to London. You see, Edward Leeford, I know all about you and your evil plan.'

'You can't prove anything!' cried Monks.

'I know every word that passed between you and Fagin,' said Mr Brownlow. 'How you plotted against Oliver. The shadows on

84

the walls caught your whispers. You are a liar and a coward. You have tried to cheat that boy – your brother. You have stolen what is rightly his – his family name and his share of his father's fortune. Do you deny any of this?'

'No – no.'

Just then Doctor Losberne was let into the room.

'What news, Doctor?' said Mr Brownlow.

'Bill Sikes' dog. It's been seen, by the river. The police are out in force. They say he can't escape. There's a hundred-pound reward on his head.'

'And Fagin? What of him?'

'He's still at large*.'

50 ∾ THE END OF BILL SIKES

In a dusty corner of a rat-infested warehouse Toby Crackit and Tom Chitling sat shivering in the dark. They were in Toby's hideout, overlooking the river.

'When was Fagin captured?' asked Tom.

'Two o'clock this afternoon,' replied Toby. 'Charley and me escaped up the chimney. They nabbed Bolter, though. If he talks – and he'll sing like a canary – then Fagin will hang, for sure.'

Tom heard a scratching noise on the stairs. It was Bull's-eye, Bill Sikes' dog. He was covered in mud, and lame*. 'What's this?' cried Toby. 'He can't be coming here. I hope he doesn't come here.'

Three hours later Sikes appeared. He sat down on the floor, with his back to the wall. 'The paper says Fagin's been caught. Is that true?' he asked.

'True,' said Toby.

'How long has the dog been here?'

'Came by itself, hours ago.'

They heard footsteps on the stairs.

'Who's that?' called Toby.

It was Charley Bates. Toby unlocked the door and let him in. When he saw Bill Sikes, his eyes blazed. 'You didn't tell me he was here!' he cried.

Bill stood up. 'Charley, there's no call for that. We've got to stick together, or we'll all hang together.'

Charley faced the murderer. 'I'm not afraid of you! If they come here looking for you, I'll give you up.'

With that, he threw himself at Sikes and knocked him to the floor. But Sikes was too strong for him. The housebreaker had his knee on the boy's throat and was about to strike him. Suddenly Toby called out, 'Quiet! Listen.'

It was the sound of angry voices. A great crowd was streaming down the narrow lane towards the warehouse. Then came a loud knocking at the door. 'Open up, in the King's name,' cried a voice.

'How strong is that door?' said Bill.

'Double locks and a chain,' said Toby.

'And the street door?'

'Lined with steel sheets,' said Toby.

Sikes went to the window and looked out. Far below the angry crowd surged* around the warehouse like a raging tide*. 'Give me that rope, Crackit!' he cried. 'They're all round the front. I can climb out of the back and be clean away.'

Sikes squeezed through a narrow skylight onto the roof of the warehouse. He clambered* up, over the steep tiles. A cry went up from the mob* below. 'There he is! On the roof!'

Mr Brownlow, who was at the front of the crush, called out, 'I'll give fifty pounds to anyone who takes Sikes alive!'

Sikes tied one end of the rope to the chimney stack. He tied a wide noose* in the other end. He was about to slip the rope around his waist and lower himself to the ground, when he

slipped and fell. He tried to grab the rope. The noose wrapped around his neck. He fell thirty feet. The rope tightened like a bow-string. There was a sudden jerk. The old chimney stack quivered with the shock. The murderer swung lifeless against the wall.

50 ᢓ OLIVER MEETS MONKS AGAIN

Two days later Oliver was taken to the town where he was born. He travelled in a coach with Mrs Maylie, Rose, and Doctor Losberne. Mr Grimwig and Mr Brownlow were waiting for them at the hotel.

After dinner Mr Brownlow said to Oliver, 'There is someone in the next room that I would like you to meet.'

The door opened and there was Monks! Oliver stared at the man in astonishment.

Mr Brownlow put his arm around the boy's shoulder. The old gentleman looked at Monks. 'This will be painful for the boy, but the truth must be told. This child is your half-brother. He is the illegitimate* son of your father, my dearest friend. His mother was Agnes Fleming. She died giving birth to Oliver in the workhouse, in this very town. Now, tell the boy what you told me. And I want the truth! Tell the truth, for once in your miserable life!'

Monks did not look at Oliver. He stared at the floor as he spoke. 'My father made a will*. He left some money to me and my mother. But most of his estate he left to Agnes Fleming and her child.'

'And what happened to that will?' said Mr Brownlow.

'My mother burnt it.'

'So you and she cheated Oliver. You stole his father's money from him.'

'Yes.'

The old gentleman then took Rose by the arm. 'This man has something to say to you now, my dear.'

'What?' asked Miss Maylie.

'Have you seen this young woman before?' Mr Brownlow said to Monks.

'Yes.'

Rose was shocked. 'But I have never seen this man before!' she said.

'Agnes Fleming had a sister. The two were separated when they were children. The young one was left alone, in poverty.'

'Until I found her, and took her in,' said Mrs Maylie.

'And became the only friend I ever had,' cried Rose. 'So, Oliver, it seems I am your aunt.'

Oliver ran to Rose and threw his arms around her. 'Rose, my dear darling Rose. I will never call you aunt. You are a sister to me!'

Then Mr and Mrs Bumble were led into the room. They looked flustered* and ill at ease. Mr Brownlow pointed at Monks. 'Do you know this man?' he asked.

'No,' said Mr Bumble. 'Never saw him in all my life.'

'Never sold him anything?'

'No, not I.'

'You are a fool. Monks has confessed*. We know all about the locket. I shall see to it that both of you are punished. You will never be employed in a position of trust again. You may go!'

Later that evening Rose was alone in her room. There was a soft tap at the door. It was Harry Maylie.

'I have heard the whole story,' he said. 'Mr Brownlow told me everything. I have come to ask you, once again, to marry me.'

'Harry!' cried Rose. 'How can you? You know my family's shameful history. Nothing has changed between us.'

Harry took her hands in his. 'You are wrong, Rose,' he said. 'Everything in my life has changed, except my love for you. I have

given up all my ambitions. I have turned away from my powerful friends. Now I have nothing to lose. Nothing to fear. I am going to be the vicar of a village church. Will you join me in my simple cottage as a vicar's wife? Will you marry me?'

'Yes,' said Rose.

52 ∾ FAGIN'S LAST NIGHT

The crowded courtroom was silent. All eyes were on the foreman* of the jury.

'Guilty!'

A tremendous shout, then another and another. Fagin would die on Monday – hanged by the neck until he was dead.

Fagin sat in the condemned cell* in Newgate Prison. There were two prison officers in the cell with him. The prisoner was never to be left alone.

On Sunday one of the jailers said, 'Fagin, there's somebody who wants to see you.'

It was Mr Brownlow and Oliver.

'You have some papers,' said the old gentleman, 'given to you by a man called Monks.'

'It's a lie,' said Fagin. 'I haven't got any papers.'

'For the love of God,' said Mr Brownlow. 'In a few hours you will be dead. Sikes is dead and Monks has confessed. What can you hope to gain by lying? Where are those papers?'

Fagin looked at Oliver. 'Come here, my dear. Let me whisper to you.'

Oliver went to him. 'The papers are in a canvas* bag, in a hole half-way up the chimney in the top room.'

Oliver and the old gentleman left Newgate Prison as dawn was breaking. A great crowd had already gathered to witness the hanging. They were drinking, smoking, and playing cards to pass

the time. There was hustle and bustle* all around. And there, in
the middle of all that noisy life, stood the black stage, the gallows,
and the rope.

53 ～ A HAPPY ENDING

Before three months had passed, Rose and Harry were married in
the village church where Harry was to work. Mrs Maylie went to
live with them in the country. Monks left England to live in
America. He died there, in prison – a fraud and a thief.

Mr Brownlow adopted Oliver as his son. The old gentleman,
Oliver, and Mrs Bedwin moved to a cottage within a mile of Rose
and Harry's home. In time, Doctor Losberne joined them. He
retired and took up gardening and fishing. Noah Claypole was

given a free pardon because he gave information to the police about Fagin and his gang. Charley Bates, shocked by Nancy's murder, turned away from crime. He left London and got a job on a farm.

Mr and Mrs Bumble were dismissed from their jobs at the workhouse. After years of misery and poverty they returned to the workhouse as paupers*.

In the old village church, not far from Oliver's new home, Mr Brownlow had a white marble slab* mounted* on the wall. On it was just one word: 'Agnes'.

GLOSSARY

3 **workhouse** place where the poorest people lived and were made to work
parish local area, centred on a church
parish child a child who is looked after by local (parish) charity
orphan a child whose parents are dead

4 **sevenpence-halfpenny** about 3p in today's money (but worth much more); 12 pence = 1 shilling, 20 shillings = £1
beadle parish official in charge of children
parlour small sitting-room
cocked hat three-cornered hat (see picture p.4)
cane elegant walking-stick

5 **pocket-book** notebook
foundlings little children who have been found deserted, with nobody to look after them
board group of officials in charge of an organization
chairman the chief official
waistcoat short coat, without sleeves

6 **trade** skill, job
ward large room where many people sleep, like in a hospital
copper large cooking pot made of copper
gruel thin food, like watery porridge
drew lots a way of choosing

someone by chance, for example using straws of different lengths
reckless without fear
ladle large spoon for serving food

8 **apprentice** young person who works with someone older in order to learn a skill or trade
pump machine used for raising (pumping) water, by hand
flogged beat
chimney-sweep person who cleans chimneys (boys were used to climb up inside the chimneys)
smothered covered and unable to breathe

9 **considered** thought about
farthing one quarter of one old penny
magistrate an official in a law court, like a judge
dotes on loves

10 **drawn and quartered** torn apart after hanging – a very nasty punishment

11 **undertaker** person who organizes funerals
terms conditions (of the agreement)
house-boy boy who works as a servant in a house
bellowed shouted; roared like a bull
blubbering crying

12 **shutters** wooden boards covering windows
close humid; sticky

13 **under me** at my command
ruffian lout
charity-boy boy who has been looked after by parish charity
washerwoman woman who washes clothes

14 **mute** boy who appears at funerals but does not speak ('mute' usually means 'unable to speak')
grate fireplace
hard on his heels following him closely

16 **coal cellar** underground room used for storing coal
ma'am madam

19 **milestone** stone by the road which tells you how far it is to the next town
turnpike-keeper person who looks after a toll-gate (where you have to pay to travel on a road)
Barnet town then north of London (now part of London)
snub nose small, turned-up nose
with a swagger confidently; showing off
lodgings somewhere to live or stay

20 **fret** worry

21 **repulsive** very unpleasant

22 **capital punishment** punishing a crime by sentencing someone to death

23 **green** innocent; not experienced
shilling coin equal to 5p (see note on p.93)

26 **lean** thin
stern serious; a bit frightening
scowl angry expression; frown
scoundrel villain; rascal

27 **hard labour** punishment involving forced physical work
fitful restless

29 **feverish** slightly fevered (hot and restless)
exclamation cry, outburst
throttle strangle
thick-set sturdy, strong, heavy

31 **blab** talk without stopping himself

32 **wretched** terrible
cause reason

34 **go down** get caught and put in prison
dingy dark; dirty
on the scent following the clues; tracking Oliver as a dog can track by smell

35 **brutal** cruel; violent

36 **barred** blocked with a wooden or iron bar

39 **inn** public house (pub)
hearty large and pleasant

40 **low** poor; bad

41 **neglect** not being looked after
menacing frightening
seldom not often

43 **melting-pot** heavy pot used for
melting metal (such as stolen
gold jewellery)

44 **when his blood's up** when he is
angry

46 **Shepperton** town west of
London
tumbledown ruined

47 **Chertsey** town further west of
London
buckle bend; crumple
crow-bar metal bar used for
forcing open doors and
windows
prised forced; levered

48 **matron** woman in charge

49 **attic** room under the roof at the
top of a house

51 **gallows** wooden structure on
which criminals were hanged

52 **by-ways** small streets
unmoved without sympathy

54 **prison colony** place where
criminals live together (in a
distant country)
bonnet hat with strings that tie
under the chin
out of sorts upset

55 **vacancy** job available

56 **bound** tied up

butler head servant
lantern lamp

57 **exhaustion** being tired
stirred moved slightly

58 **patient** person who is being
looked after by a doctor

59 **presently** in a moment
trespassing being on land that
you are not allowed to visit
gamekeeper person who looks
after the wild animals on
somebody's land
poacher person who kills wild
animals on somebody else's
land
housebreakers' robbers'

61 **niece** brother or sister's
daughter

62 **post-boy** boy who carried
letters

64 **start** sudden, surprised
movement

65 **name** reputation

68 **meek** shy; quiet

69 **ramshackle** rambling, untidy;
tumbledown
warehouse building where
goods are stored
timbers wooden beams
locket a small case holding a
picture or other precious thing,
worn around the neck
engraved written with a sharp
point in the metal

73 **identity** who he really is

agitated worried, upset

74 **drawing-room** large sitting-room where guests are welcomed

77 **mail-coaches** coaches which carried letters (and sometimes money)
   alias also known as (a false name)

78 **nabbed** arrested

79 **dejected** very sad

84 **rogue** dangerous man; criminal
   fraud lying, cheating, pretending to be someone else
   estate land and property

85 **at large** free; on the loose
   lame not able to walk properly; limping

86 **surged** moved with great speed and force
   tide flood of water
   clambered climbed, with difficulty

mob crowd
noose loop of rope with a sliding knot

88 **illegitimate** not legal (because his parents were not married)
   will written statement of what you want to happen to your possessions after your death
   flustered worried; uneasy

89 **confessed** admitted to (a crime)

90 **foreman** leader; spokesman
   condemned cell prison room for someone who is going to be hanged
   canvas strong cloth

91 **hustle and bustle** busy, excited activity

92 **paupers** very poor people
   marble slab flat piece of white stone
   mounted put in place; set